DATE DUE			
Cleland OC 21 '96			

F   Rounds, David
Rou

        Cannonball River
        tales

Butte Valley High School Library
Dorris, California 96023
916-397-4161

 Bound to Stay Bound Books, Inc.

Cannonball River Tales

Cannonball

ILLUSTRATIONS BY

A L I X   B E R E N Z Y

SIERRA CLUB BOOKS FOR CHILDREN

San Francisco

River Tales

David Rounds

for Nathaniel

The Sierra Club, founded in 1892 by John Muir, has devoted itself to the study and protection of the earth's scenic and ecological resources — mountains, wetlands, woodlands, wild shores and rivers, deserts and plains. The publishing program of the Sierra Club offers books to the public as a nonprofit educational service in the hope that they may enlarge the public's understanding of the Club's basic concerns. The Sierra Club has some sixty chapters in the United States and in Canada. For information about how you may participate in its programs to preserve wilderness and the quality of life, please address inquiries to Sierra Club, 730 Polk Street, San Francisco, CA 94109.

First Edition

Library of Congress Cataloging-in-Publication Data

Rounds, David.
    Cannonball River tales / by David Rounds ; illustrations by Alix Berenzy.
      p.   cm.
    Summary: Tall tales about Tom Terry, whose home by the banks of the magical Cannonball River is populated by a talking rabbit, a flying silver dragon, and other unusual characters.
    ISBN 0-87156-577-3
    [1. Tall tales.]   I. Berenzy, Alix, ill.   II. Title.
PZ7.R76004Can   1992
[Fic] — dc20
                                                     92-11374

Book design by Bonnie Smetts Design

Printed in the United States on acid-free paper containing a minimum of 50% recovered waste, of which at least 10% of the fiber content is post-consumer waste.

10 9 8 7 6 5 4 3 2 1

Contents

Tom Builds a Fort That Isn't Entirely

If you haven't heard tell about Tom Terry before, you won't know that he was famous all across North Dakota for his strength as a boy. All up and down the Cannonball River, which was lined with thickets of cottonwood trees, people talked about the boy who used to carry his rocking horse around on his shoulders before he was two. He told his mother it needed a rest from carrying him.

You probably think I'm exaggerating. That's exactly what people along the Cannonball River thought, if all they got was a look at Tom standing there by the water, or just wading through the wheat fields on the farm. He didn't look any different from any other sandy-haired boy with sharp eyes the color of a summer sky peering out from beneath his straw hat. You had to watch him at the age of ten, lifting up his plow and his plow mule together and flipping them around over his head at the end of the rows to save time on the turns; then you'd know that fact is stranger than fiction.

Now I know pretty much what you're thinking: that it must have been just about perfect to be strong like that as a boy. And sometimes it was. A boy or girl on a farm has got to carry in the milk pails and carry out the trash, and grind up the wheat for flour and pump up water from the well, and Tom did all that in the space between two yawns. He could read a book or beat himself at checkers while stacking bales of hay in the fall, and usually did.

But at other times, boys and girls like to roughhouse, and throw a ball or stick, and climb and jump, and slam doors on occasion. Climbing was all right, but if Tom jumped from the roof of the corncrib onto the hay cart, he broke the hay cart. If he threw a ball to a friend, the ball knocked the friend over, or maybe the barn over, if it happened to hit the barn. As for rough-housing, Tom didn't, since a broken rib on your father isn't fixed as easily as a broken rib on a hay cart. I think you'll believe me when I tell you Tom slammed a door only once. He had to hold the house up until the carpenter came.

Every day Tom's mother had to lecture him to be careful with other people, and to be careful with the animals, and not to touch this, and to leave that alone. The other boys in the valley were about as nervous around Tom as they would have been with a young bear around. It got so Tom felt like he couldn't go anywhere or do anything, except to run down to the river to build castles and forts out of stones in the current. At least the river didn't tell him to be careful.

There came a summer morning — it would have been in 1882 or '83, making Tom about ten — when a tornado happened by just to tear off the roof from the Feboldssons' barn. That was old Njal Feboldsson's place back then; he farmed a half-section, which is three hundred twenty acres, on the other side of the river from the Terry place. The roof of his barn sailed over the river and landed in the creek behind Tom's house. After a while, old Njal waded across the river with a mule team to haul the roof away. He led his mules up the creek, keeping clear of the thick wild blackberry vines that tumbled down the banks. He found his roof standing on its end in the water, with one gable in the creek and the other leaning on an arm of a cottonwood tree high overhead. Tom Terry was there, too, sitting up on the topmost point of the roof, making a drawing on a shingle with the burnt end of a broken dowel.

"Mr. Feboldsson," Tom called down when he heard the farmer coming, "are you really going to be needing this roof again?"

"Well, now," said Farmer Feboldsson, tipping his head sidewise and tugging on his earlobe, and then scratching the back of his neck beneath his long white hair, "I ain't considered much about *needing* it. I was just thinking about *hauling* it, seeing as it's in your pa's creek here, where it don't originally belong."

"It's all broken up, Mr. Feboldsson," Tom said. "I reckon the tornado wasn't being very careful. See how all them beams are snapped?" He pointed with his dowel, which he'd taken from the crumpled woodwork decorations under the eaves.

Farmer Feboldsson waded a little farther upstream and looked up into the underside of his roof. True enough, all the lumber, every length of which he'd felled with his own ax and shaped with his adz, was cracked or split or broken in two. He took a green handkerchief from a pocket in his overalls and wiped his forehead for a while. Then he said, pointing to where Tom had pointed, "Them are rafters, not beams."

"Rafters, then — but Mr. Feboldsson?" Tom said. "If you can't use this lumber again, seems to me it'd just be a load of trouble for you to haul it away. . . ." Tom ran halfway down the peak of the roof and jumped down the other half. He landed in the creek with a splash.

"Be careful, boy," said old Njal, who was actually wet enough already.

"I'm sorry," said Tom. "But look, Mr. Feboldsson." He held up the drawing he had made on the shingle. "This could be my fort. See, it's got two stories. That's the front door, and these here are windows, and that there's a trap door out onto the roof. It's got a secret door, too, except I can't show you where that is, being as it's secret. And I could build it right here in the creek, with broken lumber from your old roof — that is, if it's okay with you and my mom says I can."

Farmer Feboldsson rubbed his chin to help himself think and to keep himself from smiling. "That drawing," he said. "Mind if I take a look at it, young man?" He held it out at arm's length and studied it for a minute. "Now, this fort of yours don't show a very big roof," he said. "It's sort of tall and skinny like a grain elevator, you might say, standing up in the creek — so you ain't going to need many roofing shingles, now, are you?"

"No, sir, I ain't," said Tom, shaking in the creek with his eagerness. "I'll give you all the shingles except for the broken ones. How about that for a fair deal?"

"I'll take it, and shake hands on it," the farmer said, handing Tom back his drawing, "if you'll load the shingles."

"I'll pull 'em all off and load 'em on your cart," Tom said.

"And maybe you got time, between stints of work here, to help an old man fell some trees and trim 'em up — that is, if anybody's learned you yet how an ax fits a man's hands?"

"Mr. Feboldsson, I'll help you build your new roof *and* I'll build my fort!" Tom shouted, and he bounded down the creek all the way to the river to celebrate. The dents he made in the creekbed became the steps of a waterfall, which is still there. You can take a look at it for yourself if you don't believe me.

Tom called it Fort Cannonball. He built it over the waterfall he'd made, a few steps upstream from the meeting of the creek and the river. The fort stood on four stilts, which Tom made from the two tie beams and the two broken halves of the ridgepole of Farmer Feboldsson's roof. He hung by one arm from cottonwood branches and pounded in the stilts with a stone. I can't say the stilts made as steady a foundation as maybe they ought to have. But this was a fort for only one soldier, so Tom didn't spend much time on the foundation. He gave more care to the floor joists and the studs for the walls, which he made from the rafters of old Njal's roof.

The frame of his first floor and half the frame of his second floor were done in a week. And there the work stopped. Farmer Feboldsson's roof hadn't arrived with a floor and walls, or anything you could turn into a floor and walls. There was nothing to make a door out of, either, whether it was front or secret. Tom told old Njal about it, hoping he might have some more broken lumber stacked somewhere. But all the farmer said was "You should have planned more careful, boy. Just make it smaller."

"It's a fort, not a hut," Tom grumbled. But, as usual, grumbling didn't do any good. He waded back across the river, through the secret tunnel in the hedge of wild blackberries, past the sign that said "Fort Cannonball — Keep Out," down into the creek that fussed over the stones, and up the rope ladder to the first floor, or what would be the first floor when he found some lumber to lay one. He sat on a joist with his legs dangling in the air. The waters of the creek below him were tumbling downstream into the river and opening out there into a white fan that the river was forever brushing away. Above him, the branches of the tall cottonwoods flashed their silver leaves in the wind.

Tom didn't climb the rope ladder to Fort Cannonball the next day, or the day after. He sat on the doorstep of his farmhouse and played games of tic-tac-toe against himself by scratching with a stick in the dirt. His mother, carrying laundry, tripped over him for the tenth time and ordered him out of the yard. "Why don't you knock your silly fort down and make something useful?" she said testily, which she wasn't usually. "Build a bridge over to Febolds-sons', Tom. Or make a fence for Jeremiah." (Jeremiah was their plow mule.) "Or build me an icehouse, like a good boy. That would be nice."

She smiled down at him from over her laundry, but smiling didn't help. "Yeah, all right," Tom said, and switching with his tic-tac-toe stick at the green wheat that rose on either side of the path, he walked slowly towards the fort. He told himself he would climb up one more time, and afterwards, when he knocked it over, he wasn't going to be careful about where and how it landed.

He crawled through the tunnel in the blackberry hedge. There stood the fort, a skeleton of gray wood astride the creek. But this time, there was something odd about it. The stilts were trembling and wobbling the way they did when Tom was on the fort jumping from joist to joist. Then a *tak-tak* of hammering began clattering among the trees. Someone was in the fort; but there was no one to be seen. Tom leaped down the creekbank. "Hey!" he warned, as he swarmed up the rope ladder. "Whoever is in my fort had better be careful!"

"Oh, Tom?" called a voice, down through the floor that wasn't. The hammering stopped. "You're just in time! I've been hoping you'd come today."

It was a boy's voice. Tom paused on the ladder, but he didn't see any boy. "Where are you?" he called, and added, remembering it was his fort, "And anyway, who are you, and what do you think you're doing here?"

"I'm on the second floor. You'll see who I am! Or, well, come on up, and we'll see if you can see. I *think* you'll be able to."

Tom hurried up the rest of the ladder, and as soon as his head was above the floor joists, he heard a thump very much like the thump he made himself when he jumped from the hayloft onto the floor of the barn. There in the fort, someone who looked very much like a boy, but not entirely, was picking himself up from what would have been a landing on a floor, if there had been a floor to land on.

He was the size and shape of a boy, mostly, but his face was the bright straw-yellow of ripe wheat, and his hair rose to a high point above his face, so that his entire head seemed to be a large ear of wheat decked out with eyes, nose, and mouth. His ears, too, were two pointed shocks of wheat beside his head. His shirt and trousers were the light blue of cornflowers. He was looking wide-eyed at Tom, and then he broke into a grin when he saw how Tom was staring at him in astonishment.

"Hooray!" the boy shouted. "You can see me! It's working! It's working!" And he jumped around the fort, thumping on what by all rights had to be a floor, if a floor could be invisible.

Tom bent down and put out his hand. He felt a floorboard that his eyes couldn't see. Beyond it he felt other invisible floorboards, and the bumps on them felt exactly like the heads of invisible nails. Tom leaned on the boards; they held firm. He pushed down on them until he heard them crack; it looked to him like he was pushing on air. He turned himself around and sat down, first on the joist, then slowly on the invisible floor. He looked down through it to the creek, which was laughing by ten feet below him.

The boy who seemed to be made of wheat was squatting with his hands on his knees beside Tom. Tom said, "I reckon I can see *you*, but I can't see what you're *on*."

"I know, and I just didn't think of that, isn't that dumb? Wait, though, can you see my hammer?" The boy held up his hand, which was wrapped around something invisible. His hands and his bare feet, too, seemed built of wheat stalks grown together, and his pointed fingers and toes were set about with ripe wheat berries and soft spikes. Tom reached out to grab the invisible hammer, and he felt it and held it, but then he noticed with a shock that he couldn't feel the boy's visible hands.

Tom's fingers shook a little. "I can't feel you." He reached for the boy's arm, and he saw his fingers disappear into the blue shirt. "Hey, are you real?"

"Please don't be afraid of me, okay?" the boy said. "I'm real, but I'm just not human, is all. I'm a grain spirit, and I live in Farmer Feboldsson's hayloft. My name's Wheatberry, and I should have told you who I was right away, because my mom said you might be scared. But don't be, okay? Because that would wreck everything."

"I ain't scared," said Tom, once he found his voice. "Why ever should I be scared?"

"Good, " said Wheatberry, "because you shouldn't be." He chewed a moment on his wheat-berry fingernails and shook his head. "I just wish I could have made the fort visible for you. It would have been so much better if you could see everything."

"The fort?" Tom said, suddenly remembering the floor he was sitting on. "And just what'd you do to my fort?"

"Wait! Wait! I'm going to tell you. See, I heard everything you told Mr. Feboldsson about your fort while you were over at the barn helping him with our roof, and . . ."

Tom interrupted: "Wait, does Mr. Feboldsson know about you?"

"Well, Mom says he probably suspects. He doesn't actually *know*, I guess. But see — I don't have anybody to play with, and when I heard you telling Mr. Feboldsson how you didn't have anybody to play with, I asked my mom if somehow I couldn't let you see me. And she said no, but she said it like she wasn't absolutely sure it was no. Is your mom like that?"

"Sometimes, maybe. Not too often, I guess," Tom said. "She's kind of strict."

"My mom isn't, really. Anyway, then the other day we heard you say how you couldn't finish your fort, because you'd run out of lumber, and I asked her again. I said, couldn't I help you finish the fort with some of our own kind of materials, and no one would have to know because it's a secret and sort of in a hidden place with the blackberries and trees all around? And she said, well, she'd ask the others about it, and I guess she did, because the very next morning, which was yesterday, she said I could, for a whole month! Except we can't tell any other humans, and if any of them finds out, the fort will disappear — I mean the spirit parts of it. And I'll have to disappear, too. So I've been building for two days, waiting for you. Come on, don't you want to try it out?"

Wheatberry laughed as he watched Tom slide his feet slowly over the invisible floor and push himself carefully hand over hand along invisible walls. Wheatberry had built a second floor, too, on the skeleton Tom had made, but he hadn't hung a ladder. "Can't you jump, Tom?" he asked. With his arms by his sides, he crouched and then sprang eight feet straight up. His body passed through the solid joists. "I made a hole for you, right here. Come on, I'll help you up."

Tom chinned himself through. "Did you lay down a roof?" he asked, looking up to the clouds that were striding at a stately pace, with their chests puffed out, along the avenue of blue between the treetops. "Because it could rain."

"No, I didn't know how to build one. I figured you would."

"As it happens, I do," Tom said, as he hooked his fingers under his suspenders and snapped them to his chest. "There's some broken shingles down by the creek."

They gathered the shingles into a large pile, which Tom then bound up with a length of wild grapevine. He hoisted the bundle onto one shoulder, shinnied up a cottonwood using one arm, and threw the bundle across the creek and over the wall of the fort. The shingles crashed and scattered over the invisible floor.

Wheatberry said, "How come you could carry that whole bundle and then *throw* it?"

Tom grinned. "Throwing shingles ain't particularly special to speak of. I could throw our house a fair ways, probably. I picked it up and switched it with our barn once for April Fool's Day. My pa didn't laugh, though."

"You really did that?" Wheatberry said, doubtfully.

"Well . . . actually, I didn't. The barn might be too heavy. Then again, it might not be. I've never gone and found out how much I can lift." Tom shook his head. "The other kids say I'm not human. I am, though."

"Well, I'm not."

"It's lucky I can't touch you. If I'm not careful, people have to call the doctor after I shake hands with 'em. I couldn't begin to tell you what a bushel of trouble being strong is. Let's do the roof. You got your hammer?"

Later, when the roof was finished, Tom stood in the creek and snapped his suspenders. "Finest roof in Grant County, North Dakota." To his eye, the roof floated on the sky between the treetops like an open boat upon an upside-down river. "I wonder what Mr. Feboldsson will have to say about *this*, Wheatberry." Tipping his head to one side and pulling his right earlobe, Tom growled, " 'Well, boys, you saved on wood, and after I make my will, I might even stand under it.' "

"No, you can't tell him, Tom! We can't tell anybody!"

"Why not? How about having our moms out to watch us walk on the air? — 'Tom, be careful!' "

Wheatberry dropped down from the fort in front of Tom and laid his weightless hands on his friend's shoulders. "I already told you, don't you remember? It's got to be secret. If any human besides you finds out, I'll have to disappear right away, before our month is up."

"No, you don't. Who says? It's our fort, ain't it?"

"The River Spirit says, Tom."

"The river has a spirit?" Tom kicked a clod of dirt into the creek. "Well, I don't care about no River Spirit."

Wheatberry laughed. "You would if you met her. She's the one who said we could play together, and she showed me what to do so you could see me, which isn't something we normally ever do, you know. She said you can't let humans know about things, usually."

"Why not? What's wrong with humans knowing?"

"Don't ask me," Wheatberry said. "Some grown-up reason. It doesn't matter anyway, since we're here now, aren't we? What are we going to play?"

"Well, did you ever play Jesse James?"

"Who's Jesse James?"

"You don't know who Jesse James is? He's an extremely terrible train robber. The creek is the tracks, and he's going to ambush the train from the fort."

"Hurry up, the train's coming down the grade!" Wheatberry yelled. He sprang up to the first floor and called, "You're going to have to learn to jump, Tom. It saves time."

• • •

Tom was late for dinner that evening. "Whatever were you doing at that fort?" his mother asked, eyeing him as he slid into place at the table.

"I built a roof on it," Tom mumbled.

"A roof on it!" His mother sighed as she handed him his plate. "And here I thought you were going to do something useful."

"I was, but then I met . . ." Tom stopped himself. He chewed barley and potatoes while he considered stories that his parents would believe. "Then I found some leftover shingles, so I put a roof on. That *is* useful — in case it rains."

His father, who looked like he was never listening, but always was, said slowly, "I reckon a roof is useful, same as you're saying, if it's covering something. The only thing is, your mother told me you didn't have enough wood to even finish the frame."

"Yes, sir . . . well, I rejiggered the frame, so the roof would stay up."

Tom's mother put down her fork and fixed the fork of her gaze on him. "Tom, somebody isn't telling tall stories again? You didn't go begging wood from Mr. Feboldsson, after he'd already told you no? Or take wood from somewhere else you oughtn't to?"

"No, ma'am. No, I'm not. I didn't. The fort's fine now. Really. You can take a look yourself, if you don't believe me."

"Hmph," his mother said. "I'm not sure I do believe you, and I just might have a look."

"I'll do likewise," said his father.

Tom began to choke on his potatoes. He'd suddenly imagined his parents catching sight of the roof floating on the air. He coughed to gain time, and then said, "You couldn't get through those blackberries, I'll wager."

"No wagering in this house," his father said.

"You could part those blackberries for me with one stroke of the ax, if you had a mind to," his mother was saying at the same time.

"Oh, but I don't have a mind to. I couldn't cut the blackberries. They're the defense line. The fort is secret, Ma. Can't it be secret?"

His mother sighed.

"Can't it, Pa?" he said, looking for reinforcements. "Just for a while?"

His parents looked at each other, looked down to eat, then looked at each other again. You have to realize the difficulty Tom was working against. It was true that his mother had happened to see him carry a stalled ox across a ditch only the week before. On the other hand, he'd told her and his father so many grand fibs about traveling to Afghanistan on a flying hay bale and rafting out to Yellowstone on a subterranean river and shooting off mountaintops with his new bow and arrow that his parents didn't know when to believe him. The time came when Tom learned about the worth of the truth, but that's not part of this story.

His parents nodded to each other. "Two weeks, Tom," his mother said. "After that, we want that wood doing something useful."

"Ma, can't it be a month? Just a month? There'll still be plenty of time before school starts, and I'll build you an icehouse *and* I'll make a new fence for Jeremiah, cross my heart and hope to die if I don't."

"And where did you get the extra wood for doing both, which is what we wanted to know in the first place?"

She was smiling now, and his father looked like he wasn't listening again, so Tom knew he had his month. "Tell you what," he said. "If there isn't enough, I'll just split logs for Jeremiah. That's if there's more potatoes, please?"

Every afternoon, as the weeks hummed by, Tom and Wheatberry met at the fort to make improvements. They stripped fallen cottonwood branches to make bars for a jail cell on the second floor. Sometimes Wyatt Earp imprisoned stagecoach robbers there, and sometimes the jail belonged to the stagecoach robbers, and the robbers' hostages had to be rescued through a trap door in the roof.

Wheatberry brought some more boards to build partitions, since the United States Seventh Cavalry needed a mess hall and a soldiers' barracks and a parlor for officers. Their mounts were tied up to the stilts below, which wobbled when the soldiers fought off horse rustlers in the creekbed. With cottonwood branches, the boys built chairs for the officers and a couch for the dragon in the dragon's lair upstairs beside the jail cell. Usually he was a good dragon and guarded the prisoners, but sometimes he wasn't and ate them.

"There's supposed to be a real dragon somewhere in the valley," Wheatberry boasted to Tom, but he had to admit that no one in his family had ever seen it. "He's asleep, and only the River Spirit's allowed to wake him."

"How come?" said Tom. "I'll bet I could wake him up."

"I don't think that would be a very good idea, Tom," Wheatberry said. It turned out he was right. But that belongs in another story.

"What in goodness' name are you doing up there?" Tom's mother asked him more than once in the evening, when he'd come home wearied from a shoot-out or a siege. "Shouting and talking to yourself," she'd say, "you'd think there were half a dozen boys up there instead of one."

"Just playing robbers and dragons and things," Tom would murmur.

"Dragons? Whatever put dragons into your head?"

But she held to her bargain, and even excused him after supper sometimes, once his place was cleared. Alone on the fort, he lounged away the evenings in a floating officer's chair or on the dragon's couch. Looking down, he watched each evening sink sooner into the creekbed; he listened to the birds settle sooner into silence. Summer was leaving him. His month would soon be ending. As the colors of the earth drained away into darkness, Tom took to pacing up the creek and trudging back down again, stumbling on the shadowed stones, trying to think of a plan to make the month longer. But nothing came to mind.

The fall rains came early that year. The waters of the creek sped under the fort in a sudden hurry to reach the foaming river, and the fort leaned downstream as if to follow. Tom and Wheatberry went down to the creek to shore up the stilts with logs and stones. "My mom won't give me any more time," Wheatberry said as he waded upstream carrying a stone. The water rushed through him up to his waist. "I told you she wouldn't."

"We had to try everything," said Tom, who wasn't surprised. "Now listen. I had an idea last night. Hiking up the creek in high water is good for ideas. The day after tomorrow is our last day. We're going to have a picnic supper at the fort, and we're going to invite your ma, and my ma, and Mr. Feboldsson, and whoever else. My pa can't come that early, though, with the harvest going on." Wheatberry wanted to interrupt, but Tom interrupted him first. "I know exactly what you're going to say. You're going to say that you'll have to disappear as soon as . . . as soon as what?"

"As soon as your mom and Mr. Feboldsson come through the blackberry hedge, I guess." Wheatberry shook his head, and the berries in his crest rattled mournfully.

"So, first of all," said Tom briskly, "do you actually know how to disappear?"

"Yeah, I know," Wheatberry said, and disappeared. "See?" his voice came from the empty air. "It's easy. Wait a minute." Tom heard him mumbling. "I've forgotten how to come back! — Oh, no, I haven't." He was there again, his cornflower-blue eyes squinting in the rain. "I think your roof will fall in, too, Tom. There'll be nothing to hold it up."

"We're not allowed to be sad," Tom said, snapping his suspenders to his chest. "That's my new decision. I'm going right over to Mr. Feboldsson's tomorrow morning to invite him to a picnic supper for Thursday, six o'clock sharp at the fort, weather permitting. I'm going to help Ma make the bread. And you ask your mom. We'll get everybody together, and maybe something will happen. If it doesn't, then it doesn't. It'll be our last afternoon anyhow."

Two days later, at five minutes to six, Tom and Wheatberry were discussing their good-byes. Supper was laid out in the sun on the bank of the creek, within a moat to keep out the ants. Tom was proposing that Wheatberry come to the village school and learn to read and write; then they could send secret messages to each other on tree bark. Tom was interrupted by his mother's voice, which came from the avenue Tom had cut for her through the blackberry hedge.

"I'm sure he'd cut your blackberry vines back for you, too, Mr. F. It really isn't any trouble for him."

Tom turned his head to look, muttering, "I asked them *not* to be early." Then he heard Wheatberry's voice beside him:

"Bye, Tom."

He looked around again, and Wheatberry was gone. Tom was calling out, "G'bye! G'bye!" when the roof of the fort dissolved into a hail of shingles. They clattered down against the frame of the fort, and then splashed into the creek or fell onto the bank. Tom had covered his head with his arms, but none hit him. One of the shingles dented the stack of bread that Tom had brought. The fort was a skeleton again, just as he had built it before Wheatberry came. With no invisible floor for them to rest on, the dragon's couch was dangling by a leg from a beam, and an officer's chair was sitting upside down in the water.

"Most times I remember about," Farmer Feboldsson said, as he stood beside Tom and surveyed the litter of shingles, "people say hello when they meet, instead of good-bye. Or maybe you were saying good-bye to that roof."

"It was supposed to stay up," Tom muttered miserably.

"Ain't anything up there to *hold* it up," Farmer Feboldsson said.

"Now, Mr. F., don't tease him," Mrs. Terry said, as she took a mother's look at Tom's face. "See the lovely picnic supper he's arranged for us." She threw aside the shingle from the bread. With hands on hips, she looked up at the fort. "I'm proud that you could build something like that, Tom. May I go up on it?"

"Well . . . I guess . . . You really want to?"

"I certainly do. I've been waiting for a whole month to see it, don't forget. So mayn't I?"

Tom jumped up. "Be careful about the shingles going down to it, Ma. They got nails."

"They *have* nails," she corrected, as she took his hand and let him lead her down the creekbank.

"Wait a second." He swarmed up the rope ladder, untied it, moved it along the beam so that it hung over the bank instead of over the water, retied it, and swarmed down again.

Farmer Feboldsson was standing above them at the top of the bank. "How are those foundations, boy?"

"Okay, I think. We shored up the stilts during the rain the other day. You want to come up too, Mr. Feboldsson?"

"*We* shored them up, Tom?" his mother asked. "Was there someone helping you?"

"Yeah . . . well . . . no . . ." Tom kicked a stone or two into the water. "Just a pretend pal, I guess."

His mother patted his shoulder. She had suspected it. "Shall I go first?" she asked, catching hold of the ladder.

Tom shook his head. "I'm going to make you a place to sit." He climbed up slowly, wondering whether what he'd told his mother — that

Wheatberry was pretend — might not in fact be true. He'd meant it as an easy explanation; but now that Wheatberry was gone, it suddenly seemed impossible that he had ever come. Tom thought it must be the same as other times, when he had pretended ships that flew, or trees that did battle, or holes that made shortcuts to California. At the time, he had half forgotten that they were pretend; then suddenly he had noticed that nothing was there. And now, he guessed, he had noticed again.

Tom gathered some fallen shingles that lay about the open joists and lined them up along a beam to make a wider seat for his mother. He pressed the nails home with his thumb. "Here, Ma."

She climbed up and arrived beside him. "Thank you, dear. It's lovely up here, isn't it? You can see the creek going down into the river."

"Yep, and you can see the Feboldssons' barn from the second floor," Tom said. "Want to come up and see your barn, Mr. Feboldsson?" he called down.

"No, sir," the old man said. "I saw it pretty recent, and I ain't as young as your ma is." He was standing below them in the creek; his thick fingers were spread around one of the stilts, which trembled under his grip. "Emily," he called to Tom's mother, "I think you'd better come down. These posts can't carry much weight."

But holding lightly onto the upright studs, which were all there were of walls, she was already stepping from joist to joist towards the rope ladder to the second floor. "I'll be down in a minute, Mr. F. I just never can resist a view." She took hold of the ladder. "I'd love you to build a window in the attic,

Tom." As she stepped onto the first and then the second rung of the ladder, her weight high up on the downstream side of the fort suddenly pulled one of the stilts on the upstream side loose from its foundation. The stilt jerked upwards, and the ladder began to swing. Tom and Farmer Feboldsson shouted at the same time:

"Ma, be careful!"

"Emily, get down from that!"

"Yes . . . all right . . ." As she swung back in the direction of the loose stilt, it sank back into its hole. Then she swung again towards the downstream side. "I can get down here," she called. But before she could move, her swinging weight drew the loose stilt out of the ground again. The entire fort shifted and twisted. Then the stilt crashed shuddering down among the stones outside of its foundation. Immediately the second upstream stilt tore up from its hole, and the fort began to tip over downstream.

Balancing on the moving floor joists, Tom had been working his way towards his mother, but now he dropped to the ground, scrambled on all fours to the second stilt, wrapped his arm around it, and held it steady. "I'll stop it, Ma!"

The fort did not fall, but began twisting and shifting as the first stilt scraped and hopped beside its foundation. Farmer Feboldsson walked up to it and embraced it, but it threw him to the ground. Tom's mother was now swinging in a circle, and her weight was pulling the fort apart. She kicked out at the wall studs to stop herself as she passed them, but instead, her motion made her twist wildly as she revolved. A loud crack of a splitting beam shot out like a rifle.

"Ma! Ma!"

"Jump, Emily! You've got to jump!"

As she was watching for a moment to jump through the studs, suddenly her body jerked and slowed, making a smaller circle; then jerked again
and began spinning slowly in place; then stopped. "Tom! Something's holding
on to me!"

"It's Wheatberry! Hooray!"

"Emily, get down! It's going to fall!"

Suddenly they could see Wheatberry and his mother standing beside
the ladder, each of them with an arm around Tom's mother at the waist. With
the opposite hand, they were bracing themselves against an upright stud. Amid
sharp creaks of wrenching nails, the downstream side of the fort was slowly
leaning over, tearing itself apart from the upstream side, which Tom still held
below.

"Quickly, Mrs. Terry," Wheatberry's mother said.

Dazed from her ride on the ladder, Tom's mother did not move. She
stared at Wheatberry's mother's yellow-golden face and her hair that rose to
a point like a shock of grain.

"Hurry, Ma! That's Wheatberry and his mom! They're my friends!"

The spirits pulled on Mrs. Terry's arms. Thought returned to her eyes.

"Yes. Thank you," she said.

"Climb through and hang by your arms and then drop," Wheatberry's mother said quietly.

"Yes." She knelt on a floor joist, then lowered herself down onto her elbows. She looked up at Wheatberry's mother, who was bending over her. "But you, too!"

"It can't hurt us. Get down now. Tom! Come catch her!"

Tom left his stilt and leaped down under the fort as his mother hung from the joist and then let go. He caught her under the arms and, holding her high, waded in a run back upstream. At the same time, the fort, freed from Tom's hold, folded over with a screech of pulled nails and an explosion of cracking lumber. It crashed into the creek with its stilts in the air.

Tom sat down on the creekbank with his arm around his mother, who was shivering. Below them, Farmer Feboldsson crossed the creek and reached up the bank.

"Give me a hand up, Tom, and I'll go fetch your ma a blanket."

"No, never mind, Mr. F. I'll be all right. Just give me a minute."

They waited in silence. Then suddenly she looked down the creek at the wreck of the fort. "But they're gone!"

"They popped out of sight as soon as you jumped, Emily."

"They're probably still here, though, I'll bet," Tom said.

"They are?" She looked around her.

"You can't see them, Ma, except when they want you to. They live in your hayloft, Mr. Feboldsson. They're grain spirits."

"In my hayloft," Farmer Feboldsson repeated, smiling and rubbing the back of his neck under his white hair. "Well, I'll be pickled."

"Wheatberry said you suspected."

"He did, did he? Well, I suppose I've had the feeling that I had company up there sometimes." Tom's mother was shivering again. "Now, sir," the farmer said, "I think you should get your mother home. She needs a warm drink and some rest."

They stood up. "But your lovely picnic, Tom. And I'm sorry I ruined your fort."

"You didn't, Ma. Wheatberry had to disappear anyway, and we were saying good-bye when you came, remember?" He repacked the supper into the bushel basket he had brought it in, saying, "He didn't tell me his ma was coming to see the fort, too."

"It seems she *is* our friend," Mrs. Terry said.

"Of course. I told you she was. Why shouldn't she be? Are you coming for supper, Mr. Feboldsson?"

Tom's mother wanted him to build the fort again, but he was against it. He said there wouldn't be enough manpower for a garrison, "and besides, the bad guys have all retreated to Montana." He cleared the creek and built a fence for Jeremiah, with whatever lumber was still sound. As to whether he saw Wheatberry again, that summer or any summer after, I can't say. Tom never let on, to me at least. He wasn't one to tell you anything that he didn't have a mind to tell.

I do know for certain, though, that Mrs. Terry got her icehouse. It stood down near the creek in the shade of the cottonwoods, stacked full of ice that Tom would saw out of the river in March. All you could see of the icehouse was the shingles of the roof; there weren't any walls to hold them up — at least none that you could know about by looking. In the late summer afternoons, the hot sun would shine at the blocks of ice, but the ice would be in shadow. If you reached in to chop off a sliver of ice for your sarsaparilla, something that felt like wood would block your hand. You had to feel around for the door.

People came from all over Grant County to stare at Mrs. Terry's ice-house with invisible walls. One year someone took a chisel to it and walked off with a piece of wall to exhibit at the county fair for a nickel a rub. Afterwards, Tom put up a sign saying, "Beware of Dog — Keep Out." When I was about as old as Tom was when he built the icehouse, I went to see it for myself, since I knew Tom never had a dog; and if the blackberries haven't overgrown it, you can see it still.

Tom Changes
His Eating Habits

Tom grew up, and for a long while he didn't have time for grain spirits, or any other kind of spirits — he was too busy working the farm. In the wintertimes, when the fields were dozing under the snow, Tom took to wandering around the Dakotas to show off his strength to whoever would watch. He didn't mind at all making people's eyes pop half out of their heads and their jaws flap open when they saw him lifting things no one else could lift and carrying things no one else could carry. He'd also boast a few fibs for good measure, when he thought he could get away with it. It got him into trouble, too, but that was later, and it doesn't come into this story.

Wandering around the way he did, and living by himself, Tom had no choice but to teach himself to cook. In fact, he bragged he could cook even better than he could lift — but I don't advise you to believe it. Still, his rabbit stew did take second place one year in the bake-off at the state fair, even though the rules confined the entries to fruit pies. That's how he met his wife, Mary: she'd won first prize. Everyone but the judges said that Tom's stew was better than her apple and plum tart, and maybe it was; I couldn't say. I never got a taste of it. He stopped making it before my time. No one else could make it after him, either, since he'd never admit to the recipe. All he'd say, if you asked him, was "Eat up before the juice dries and the fork sticks to your plate." You could never get a thing out of Tom, except when he was pleased to tell you.

Now when Tom was still a fancier of rabbit, and when he'd feel the need of some of that second-prize-winning rabbit stew on his tongue, he'd just pull on his wading boots and step across his fields to the banks of the Cannonball River, which were lined with tall stands of cottonwood trees. He'd stomp through the blackberry thickets and clomp down the riverbank and barge into the current to wade upstream. You could see him splashing there, in his dark blue overalls, red woolen shirt, and yellow straw hat; he had a big drooping moustache the color of his hat and little sharp eyes the color of his overalls. He'd have his shotgun parked on his shoulder. He wasn't ready to shoot rabbit yet. First he'd charge off upstream, kicking his way against the quick black current and bellowing bits of hymns at the top of his voice — he had a fairly large voice for his size of man. I'm not going to tell you of the time he challenged a grizzly bear to a roaring contest and deafened the poor beast. He was so sorry afterwards that he took the grizzly to the ear doctor in Minneapolis. But that isn't part of this story.

Naturally, whenever the rabbits who lived at the tops of the cottonwood trees heard Tom Terry's racket come howling up the river, they'd never fail to stop munching the leaves they'd been nibbling. They'd shove the leaves aside, each with its right hind foot, and they'd take a look below. Don't ask me why: maybe they wanted to hear better what hymn Tom was singing. Down off his shoulder came Tom's shotgun, and *blam-blam-blam-blam-blam*! Inside of five seconds, five brace of dead rabbit were plummeting through the air on their way to his rabbit pouch. He was a wizard with a shotgun, Tom was. His mother used to say that the day he was two years old, he shot out the candles on his birthday cake with the corks of two vinegar bottles, at a distance of fifty yards. She may have been exaggerating; I couldn't say.

Now I know what you're thinking: rabbits don't live at the tops of cottonwood trees, or at the tops of any other trees that you've ever heard of, so how could Tom have shot rabbits out of them? You could be right, and I'm not going to argue with you, except to remind you that you weren't there, and neither was I. But I will grant you this: every year the rabbits in the trees along the Cannonball River got scarcer. It might have been because Tom Terry shot down thirty or forty of them every time he waded up the river, so as, he said, to justify his trouble. Of course he shared the extra stew with his neighbors, out of generosity and in order to collect the compliments. By the time Tom and Mary got married, though, the rabbits had just about disappeared from the trees. Tom found himself splashing his way farther and farther up the river to find a mess of rabbit to cook up for his bride.

One dry afternoon, far up the river, Tom took a turn into a bend that he didn't recognize. He told me afterwards he could have sworn the river ran straight all down that country. But there was the river curving, beneath a tall grove of ancient cottonwood trees. Their silver-leafed branches met far above the shaded water. As Tom was drawing breath to start hollering his hymns, he distinctly heard someone calling out his name behind him.

"Mr. Terry?"

Tom looked around. He couldn't see anyone.

"Hallo, Mr. Terry?"

There it was again, coming from somewhere above him: the high voice of a girl or a young boy.

"Speaking," boomed Tom, and he scanned the trees for the source of it. After a minute he noticed a shaking and a rustling high up in a particularly tall and ancient cottonwood, which grew by the bank in the inner curve of the river bend. Hopping down among the silver leaves, from thick limb to thick limb, was a jet-black rabbit a good deal larger than Tom had ever seen, with white hieroglyphical markings on his cheeks and his brow.

"Is that Mr. Terry there?" came the high, rather squeaky voice again. It was the rabbit's voice; there was no disputing it. The sound came from where he moved, and his mouth formed the words. The rabbit hopped to the ground and walked up the bank towards Tom, using just his two long black hind feet, kicking one foot up in front of the other. "Mr. Tom Terry?" said the jet-black rabbit.

"Himself," said Tom, from the middle of the river, with the current rushing by him. He was too dumbfounded to say more.

The rabbit kick-walked up the bank until he was opposite Tom, turned sideways to show the white markings around his right eye, and said in his high, nasal, rather squeaky voice: "Fire away, sir."

It's not that Tom had a slow mind, now. I don't want you to think that slowness of mind was the reason he stood there speechless, with his arms hanging slack at his sides and his shotgun butt trailing in the water. It was just that he wasn't used to seeing jet-black rabbits with white markings on their faces, or any other color of rabbit for that matter, except a brown sort of gray, or maybe a gray sort of brown. He wasn't used to seeing rabbits hop down to the ground and kick-walk up the riverbank, either, and he wasn't much used to hearing rabbits talk English, especially dictionary English. In fact, he'd never seen or heard tell of any one of these things.

But Tom wasn't the kind of man to show his surprise for long, if he could help it; it didn't sit right with his principles. His wife, Mary, used to say that when the tornado of '98 snatched up their house and set it down politely on the roof of the Grant County courthouse, then snatched the house up again and set it down home where it belonged, except slightly skewed around, Tom didn't even bother to get up from his breakfast to look out at the sights flying by below. "His knee trembled a bit on the way down," Mary said. But Tom denied it. "I always did want the kitchen facing the barn, so I could hear the cows better while I was eating," was all he'd say about it.

The rabbit stood patiently on the riverbank, without the faintest touch of trembling about his black nose. "Well, Mr. Rabbit, sir," Tom said at last, pulling himself together and tipping his straw hat politely. (He told me afterwards that this was how he guessed a man ought to talk to a talking rabbit. "My ma used to say to me, 'Tom, if you don't know who he is, then he's your better,' " is how he explained it.) "Well sir, Mr. Rabbit," said Tom, then, "if you'll excuse me, I don't believe I can shoot you. Not like this, in cold blood; it ain't right."

"I beg your pardon," said the rabbit rather sharply. "*Your* calling *me* cold-blooded is just a little bit funny, considering your usual bloodthirsty activities on this river. I'll thank you to take aim, sir." The rabbit turned sideways again, and his large left eye watched Tom calmly.

"No offense meant, Mr. Rabbit," Tom said, feeling a little confused. "In cold blood, that's a manner of expression, see. It means you don't shoot a thing that can't defend itself or run for cover. A man has his principles."

"Ah," said the rabbit, with relief in his voice. "That's all right, then. You'll pardon me for not understanding your principles. I'll run for the trees, and you'll shoot — will that be satisfactory?" And he turned around briskly and hopped in long, high bounds down the riverbank.

Tom raised his gun in order to fire. Then he pointed the gun down again. It was one thing to shoot a dumb animal and eat it, he told himself, but how was he going to cook up a stew from a rabbit that had called him by his name, with "mister" and "sir" added on politely?

The rabbit was kick-walking back along the bank. "Well?" he said irritably when he stopped across the current from Tom. "Did you run out of ammunition — or principles?"

"No sir," said Tom, "and no offense, but I just don't see how I can shoot you." He stowed his rifle firmly under his arm, to show he'd made up his mind — "which a man has to do," as he said to me afterwards, "even if he don't know what the devil is going on."

"Hmph," the rabbit grumped, twitching his whiskers fussily. "And might I ask *why* you can't shoot me?" he asked, in the sharp, examining voice of a schoolteacher or a judge.

"I reckon you might," Tom said slowly, to gain time, since he didn't generally approve of giving his reasons. He liked having the last word in an argument, which you don't always get if you're willing to explain yourself. But the truth was that he wasn't ready for the last word; he wasn't ready to wake up, in case this was a dream. He wanted to find out who the black rabbit was, and what his purpose was in asking Tom to shoot him. Better than food or money, Tom loved a brisk debate on any subject whatever, including subjects he didn't know much of anything about. He especially loved discussions with the out-of-the-ordinary characters who happened into the Cannonball Valley now and then, such as peddlers of ointments and shoes, and preachers and politicians, and also — well, he might have been remembering Wheatberry, too, right about then, though he didn't mention it afterwards.

"Mr. Rabbit," he said finally, "I can't shoot you because" — here Tom hooked his thumbs under his suspenders and snapped them to his chest, to show that he was feeling free and comfortable — "if I'm awake on the river here, I won't shoot anyone who's capable of friendly conversation. And if I'm dreaming in my bed, I might kick the missus on the recoil."

"Hmph," the rabbit said. "You've shot most of my friends without engaging *them* in conversation. So," he added grimly, "it's perfectly all right to shoot anyone who doesn't talk. But it's wrong to shoot someone who does. I gather that's another of your interesting principles? Very educational, though I can't say I see the logic in it."

"It's got logic in it there somewhere for certain, Mr. Rabbit, take it from me," Tom said smoothly. He was making sure to be smiling calmly, because he wanted to hide the bother being caused in his mind by a certain troubling thought. It bothered him enough to make him set aside one of his debating principles, which was never to admit to not knowing something. "Them friends of yours," he asked, clearing his throat, "I reckon they aren't of the talking variety, like yourself, though, are they? Except for a rabbity sort of squeak now and then, and a thump or two of the hind foot?"

"How would you know if they could talk or not, since you've never bothered to ask them before you shot them?" the rabbit said, thumping his hind foot impatiently. "Did you ever meet a tree spirit that *couldn't* talk?"

"Tree spirits," Tom mumbled. He was feeling a little unhappy in his stomach.

"Well, didn't you know we were tree spirits?" the rabbit asked scornfully. "Did you actually suppose we were rabbits? This is really beyond belief. If we were rabbits, how could we be living in trees?"

Tom couldn't think of anything for an answer — a situation he wasn't in the least bit used to. He took off his hat, soaked his handkerchief in the river, and doused his hot forehead with the cool water.

"If you want to know," the tree spirit who looked like a rabbit continued, "tree spirits are always looking down from their trees to see who might be passing by in the mood for a talk. I keep telling them there's no hope in it where *you're* concerned." The tree spirit sighed and twitched his nose. "Well, sir," he said, after waiting a while, "since you have nothing to add, I'll take my leave." He turned around and kick-walked his way back along the bank to the tall and ancient cottonwood tree at the inner curve of the river bend. He hopped onto a low limb, hopped onto a higher limb, and was gone among the shimmer of silver leaves.

Tom walked home that day without knowing he was doing it. "The cool air under those trees put me into a kind of sleep," he said afterwards. It wasn't until he got home, and Mary asked him why he was out in the garden digging turnips when it was time to cook up some rabbit, that he suddenly remembered what had happened. He told her about it, and she asked him if he wasn't feeling well. She might have persuaded him that he'd dreamed it all, too, or that his head had been turned by a touch of sun, if he hadn't noticed the next morning that the butt of his shotgun was warped. You remember I told you that he let it trail in the river when the jet-black rabbit first dumbfounded him by calling out his name.

"I had to go back there and find him," Tom explained to me afterwards. "I had to tell him how shamed I felt about what I did to his friends. I was also fixing to ask him why tree spirits live along the river and why nobody else seems to see them excepting me. Here I'd been wondering about those tree rabbits all my life, and when I had a chance to find out about them, I forgot to ask. Besides, you never could tell: maybe he knew what the cows talk about in the barn at night. I was always wondering about that, too."

So Tom trudged up the river again. But the bend with the grove of ancient cottonwood trees wasn't there to be found. Tom walked miles beyond where he thought the bend had been, and miles back again, but the river ran straight all down that country. He looked up and down the Cannonball Valley for three days. At every particularly tall and stately cottonwood, he stopped and called up the trunk: "Mr. Tree Spirit, sir! If you're there, I'd be mightily pleased by some polite and peaceable conversation!" Or he'd say, "Mr. Tree Spirit, sir! I don't have my shotgun with me, just take a look!" He'd hold up his hands to show they were empty. But no squeaky voice came in answer.

From those three days, Tom came back home sore-throated and weary-legged and a changed man. He never shot a living thing afterwards. He wouldn't have a gun in the house. "I can't know who I might shoot," he told his missus. "It might be someone like him." At night you could sometimes hear Tom out in the barn, chatting with the cats and swapping stories with the cows. If you laughed about it, he tended to get testy. "They'd talk to you, too, if they thought you'd listen," he'd say.

That same year Tom entered his savory turnip-and-greens stew in the bake-off at the state fair, and won it, too. Mary said the secret was the dillweed she'd spied him sneaking in from the garden. But he wouldn't admit to it. "I save on buckshot," was all he'd say, "and I never felt better in my life."

Tom Keeps a Promise

I've already told you how Tom liked to boast about his strength to everyone who'd listen, and also to some who wouldn't. He was always testing how much stretch there was in any part of the truth that looked to be elastic. There wasn't any need for him to exaggerate, though, considering what he could already do — that was the funny part about it. I went with him myself one time when he hoisted two of his cows onto his shoulders and carried them all the way to Bismarck to see the foot doctor there — a distance of about sixty miles. Their hooves were so infected they couldn't walk. Tom's hands weren't free, so I went along to do the milking. He never put the cows down once till we got to the doctor's office; he told me he didn't want to move them once they'd gotten comfortable.

Of course, that foot doctor in Bismarck was so curious to investigate Tom and make some tests and perform some experiments concerning Tom's strength that he completely forgot about the cows. Tom kept them on his shoulders till a big enough crowd had gathered round. Then he said, "Cows aren't particularly heavy to speak of. You might want to know about the time a tornado dropped in on the Cannonball Valley and twisted the weather vane on top of the water tower at Mrs. Granville's apple farm so the arrow pointed south instead of north. She asked me to put it right for her and brought me a ladder, but I couldn't spare the time to climb it, and I don't take to heights. I just hefted the whole water tower up from the ground and turned it around a half turn so the arrow pointed north again. There isn't much to picking up water towers, either. I'll thank you for seeing to my cows, Doctor, and for a glass of Vichy water to lubricate the talking-organ."

I asked Tom afterwards where Mrs. Granville lived, since I'd never heard of her before.

"There ain't any Granvilles in the Cannonball Valley, and there ain't any apple farms, either," Tom said, hooking his thumbs under his suspenders and snapping them to his chest. "But you saw how they believed me anyway." I didn't trouble to ask him why carrying two cows wasn't enough for him. He always liked to spin things out for the effect.

I never saw Tom trouble himself for one minute to build up his strength, which came to him ready-made when he was born. But his boasting and his fast talking were different; he learned them out of hard practice. Not too many nights would pass without his pulling on his wading boots and stepping across his fields to the banks of the Cannonball River, lined with blackberry thickets beneath the silver-leafed cottonwood trees. He'd stand in the current or wade upstream, all alone in the dark, with the rushing of the river and the rustle of the leaves in the night wind, and he'd dream up stories to tell people and quick answers to silence people with in the morning. He'd rehearse them out loud, with the river as his audience, to get them down smooth and right.

"I used to listen to the water, too, so as to get the idea of how it sounded to be a master talker," he told me once. "The river never stops to think, but every minute it has some new thing to say." He thought maybe if he could just listen a bit harder, a little bit more carefully, he'd be able to understand the river's words.

Now when Tom and Mary had been married three years or there-abouts, a wet spring came to the Cannonball Valley. The river rose high with the rains, and one night it tore out some trees along the bank. They fell into the current and backed up the water. The river started flowing out onto the already saturated fields. The next morning, Tom pulled on wading boots and hitched himself up between his two plow mules. Knee-deep in mud, the three of them dragged the trees out of the stream and freed the river.

A crowd of neighbors gathered around to watch. That's what Tom couldn't resist. When the last big limb was hauled out onto the bank, he un-hitched himself from the harness and said, "Trees aren't particularly heavy to speak of, especially when a feller's got previous experience. Before I was a married man, I used to pick up pocket money riding the paddle wheelers on the North Platte River in Nebraska. I'd rig me up a seat right down there in front, just below the statue of the lady on the bow. Wherever there was a snag in the channel, or a fallen tree or a boulder or a sandbar or a small island or maybe an alligator or a hippopotamus in the water up ahead there, I'd just reach down and flip it aside. The captain wouldn't have to even nudge the rudder. He could sleep up there on the bridge and often did. As for this little Cannonball here, why, if it was piled two hundred feet high with cottonwood trees, and every one of them measured fifty feet around at shoulder level, I could clear it out in half a morning, and that's a promise."

Miss Latham, who taught down at the schoolhouse, said there weren't any hippopotamuses on the North Platte, and she didn't believe there were any alligators in it, either. Tom snapped his suspenders to his chest and didn't skip a breath. "Of course there aren't, Abigail. I flipped them all out of there long ago." I suspect he'd practiced that answer in advance.

Tom particularly favored his story about riding the paddle wheelers on the North Platte. That spring, just about everybody in the valley got to hear the story quite a few more times than once. His missus suggested it was getting stale, and he told her that he knew it was, but that he couldn't think of anything to top it. He took to spending two and three hours a night wading up the Cannonball deep in thought, but nothing came to him.

One evening, when it seemed to him he'd waded far beyond the spot where he usually turned around, he suddenly noticed that less and less current was washing around his knees. Before long, the river was only a few feet wide, and it was just splashing around the toes of his boots, shallower than he'd ever seen it, even in a dry summer. But it wasn't summer yet, and there had just been four days of rain.

He stopped and looked around him in the starlight; that night, there was no moon. On either side of him, the river bottom was naked mud, all cluttered with stumps and stones and broken limbs, as if the river upstream had been stopped with a dam. As he walked on slowly in the dark, branches whipped his face, and he stumbled on roots. He had just about decided he was going to have to turn around, though he still hadn't thought of any new stories to tell, when he noticed that the current was silent altogether. Before him was a wide pool, clear and still. The clutter of stumps and fallen trees was gone. On the shore at his feet was smooth sand.

There in the center of the pool, maybe twenty feet from where he stood, a little spring bubbled up from the surface of the water. The spring was filled with light, and it made no sound, so that Tom thought at first it must be the moon's reflection broken into fragments on the water. But this night, there was no moon. The air was filled with a sweet smell that he couldn't name. He stood wondering.

Suddenly the pool began to fill with a strange, quiet, silver light, first underneath the water, so that he could see the clear bottom, and then above the water, so that he could see the riverbank on either side, and the low branches of the trees hanging over the water, and his own feet standing on the golden sand. Only the far shore beyond the pool was left in darkness. He felt weak and strange. Then he heard:

"Tom?"

He looked around; there was no one.

"Tom Terry?"

There it was again, a woman's voice, seeming to call from the spring at the center of the pool.

"It is Tom Terry, isn't it?"

There was no disputing it: the voice came from the spring, as if some-one were there hidden in its light. As soon as he had that thought, he saw a woman standing on the spring. Its current of light seemed to flow down through her straight black hair, ripple through her long blue robes from her shoulders to her bare feet, and then spill from her feet onto the surface of the pool, as if she herself were the source of the spring.

He couldn't guess how old she was. Her face was as clear and bright as a young girl's, but in her eyes was the knowledge of great age. She looked at Tom with an expression of laughing kindness. "We were glad to hear you coming," she said.

Tom didn't know what to say, which was just as well, since he didn't have any voice to say it with.

Slowly she turned her head, and as she looked behind her and above, the light around her flowed back to the far shore, till Tom could see what had backed up the river. Stumps and fallen cottonwoods, piled in a jumble, lay like a dam in the river's path. Here and there water seeped through the dam in a trickle to form the pool. As she looked up and up, her light rose against a wall of trees, some of them thicker than he'd ever seen — fifty feet around at shoulder height, with upended stumps fifteen feet across. Higher and higher they were piled — eighty, a hundred feet, higher than the tops of the trees still standing on the banks, still higher, an enormous dark shape two hundred feet high, till at last he could see the stars shining through the branches at its crown.

She looked back at Tom, with the dam still lit behind her. "Will it really take you only half a morning to clear it out?" she asked.

Tom wasn't over being stunned, but he had a hunch it was time to get out of there, or else be stuck with the need for some fast-talking that he hadn't had time to rehearse. He took off his yellow straw hat and nodded politely. Then he put his hat back on again. "Well, ma'am, " he said, "I've been honored to meet you, but the cows don't like to be kept waiting." He turned around to go, but he'd only taken one step when he heard her pure voice not far behind him:

"Tom?"

Slowly he turned around again. She had crossed the water without a sound and was standing there a few feet down the shore from him.

"There are only trees here," she said. "No alligators, and no hippopotamuses."

Tom hooked his thumbs in his suspenders. He told me later that, right at first, he'd felt kind of pleased to hear how far his North Platte paddle wheeler story had been circulating around. At the same time, he didn't see what point this fine lady thought there was in making jokes about it.

"Now, you see, ma'am," he said to her, "clearing away a big pile of debris like you've got here — being a lady you might not know how it goes about being done, but you'll need six, maybe eight or ten ox teams, and a team of men with axes. It's a couple weeks' work at least. That's a lot of cordwood up there. You've got to move real carefully, considering all the water that's probably backed up behind it."

"Two weeks," she repeated. "And teams of oxen and men." She nodded her head, and the single blue gem bound by a cord to her forehead flashed in the night. "I really did wonder if you could do it as easily as you promised."

"You didn't tell *me* that," a nasal, rather squeaky voice called out from a tree down the shore. "You said you were sure he *could* do it."

"I wanted to believe it," she said, turning and smiling as a large tree limb bent down slowly over the water, and what looked like a large, jet-black rabbit hopped off the limb and onto the sand. He waved a paw at the tree, and the limb rose up again without him.

"You have met my friend Theodore before," the lady observed.

"Yes" — Tom cleared his throat — "Yes, ma'am." He took off his hat to nod to the tree spirit, but despite more throat clearings, he couldn't bring out a greeting. He dropped his hat without noticing.

"Hmph," Theodore said, looking Tom up and down sternly. "I told the Princess it would be a waste of time to call you — although I certainly wouldn't have minded being pleasantly surprised."

"It wasn't a waste of time when you called him before," the Princess reminded him. "He hasn't brought his gun up the river since you did."

"He hardly had a choice, since there were hardly any of us left for a while to shoot," Theodore said, crossing his rabbit arms and thumping his hind foot.

But the Princess was smiling as she said to Tom, "You can see that you've been the subject of an argument between friends. Theodore thinks you can't change. I think you can."

Tom stood straight, squared his shoulders, and found his voice. He could see that the Princess's side of the argument was favoring him and that it needed some defense. "I smashed my gun, Master Theodore," he said, "and I didn't get me another. I looked for you to tell you how right sorry I was."

"You see?" the Princess said, looking down at Theodore.

"I make a turnip stew now, which is thicker and as tasty as the rabbit," Tom added for good measure, and then doubted if he should have said it, since it hadn't come out sounding necessarily like a compliment.

The spirits made no answer; they seemed to be waiting. The night held the pool in stillness. After a minute Tom felt he had to fill the silence, in order to keep in charge of the conversation. "Ma'am, if I could ask . . . ?" He stopped short; that wasn't how he liked to begin.

"Yes, Tom?"

"What I mean is, I somehow missed my directions in the dark back there, and it might be a help if I knew where I was, seeing as how I'm to get some folks together to clear the mess out of the river here."

"We are on your farm," the Princess said, "not a quarter of a mile from your house."

Tom raised his hand to fan himself with his hat, until he found that it wasn't in his hand. He looked down and spotted it on the sand, stooped to pick it up, fanned himself a minute, widened his stance a notch, and said, "Well, ma'am, I don't mean to contradict, but I don't see how that can be. I've been over every inch of the river from the village to the falls, and I've never seen this place before, I promise you."

"Hmph: your promises," Theodore snorted. "They come cheap."

"Now, Theodore, how is he to know?" the Princess said. "My pool is a spirit place, Tom. You can't see it, even if you're standing in it, unless we call you."

Tom was feeling watery-kneed again. He looked up to her face, and now he could see clearly that the light that shone in the night flowed directly from her. Light, not water, was the current that rippled through her face and down her hair and her robes. As she watched him, he thought that her light must be shining through him as through glass. "Who are you?" he said.

"I am the River Spirit, Tom," she said. "Have you never heard of me?"

Tom remembered his friend Wheatberry telling stories about her, though he hadn't completely believed them at the time. He mumbled, "Yes, ma'am, I reckon, once or twice."

"Didn't you say you wanted to hear the river's words?"

"Yes, ma'am. Yes, I did."

"Her words have something to do with that pile of trees over there, if I'm not mistaken," Theodore remarked, rather sharply as it seemed to Tom.

Tom swallowed, and worked on keeping his knees stable. "I don't know if I can get a work crew out here, though. If I tell 'em, they might not believe me, see . . . no offense, but . . ." He didn't finish.

"You cannot bring them here," the River Spirit said. "You can only clear the river by yourself."

Again the spirits were silent. As the quiet seconds passed, Tom's hands sunk into his pockets, and his glance rose to the dam beyond the pool, then fell to his boots. "Well, of course," he said at last, shoving some sand around with his toe, "this business of what I told everyone, of it maybe taking half a morning to clear out a dam like this one here all on my own — it was all just talk, see. It don't necessarily mean a man can actually do it." He turned his hat around in his hands. "If I'd given my word to do it, that would have been

one thing. But as I was just making it up for people to hear — " He kicked sand
into the pool with a small splash. "Just boasting about a thing isn't the same as
giving your word to it. I think you ought to know that."

Suddenly the light at his feet began to fade. He looked up quickly.
He could still see them there, but dimly. The River Spirit's light shone faintly,
and in her face alone. "Never mind, then, Tom," she said. "Good night."

The light slipped away from the shore. In the dimness he heard the
rustle of a branch descending over the pool, then rising again. The light gathered into the spring at the center of the pool, sparkled there quietly for a long
moment, and then went out. The trees around him stepped back into the dark
of the night.

For a long time Tom stood there without moving. He told me afterwards that he'd never expected them to leave so quickly. He suddenly realized
that something as peaceful and pure as the River Spirit's light, something like
joy, had been rising like a spring in his mind all the while she had been shining
there. But he had scarcely noticed it, until it was gone. He had been too busy
arguing.

Now a thousand questions he could easily have asked the spirits
poured into his mind, questions he had been hoping all his life to find someone
to answer: not only who the river was, and what the river knew, but who he
himself was, too, and where he had come from to be born into the Cannonball
Valley, and where he would go when he would die. He'd had his chance to
learn, maybe, and all he'd done was make excuses. He began calling out to
the spirits, turning around this way and that to the pool and the trees. "Ma'am?
Mr. Theodore? Are you here? Ma'am?" But no spirit voices came in answer.

At last he began walking slowly, around the shore towards the dam. He climbed up the face of it, always careful not to look down, since he'd never taken much to heights. Now and then, when he had a hand free, he hooked a thumb under a suspender and snapped it to his chest to work up some courage. The River Spirit had said she'd wanted to believe that he could keep his word, and it wouldn't be respectful, he told himself, it wouldn't sit right with his principles, to let her down. Besides, it was out of the question to let Theodore win the argument.

He reached the top of the dam, and he began throwing down trees and stumps onto the fields below. He told me afterwards that many of the trunks were far too heavy for him to lift, but he'd decided he didn't care; he'd lift them up anyway. He'd picture in his mind how he'd seen the River Spirit standing on the shore of the pool, with the cascade of light spilling silently down her robes, and he'd heave at the trees, thinking of her instead of them.

Once he'd thrown down about fifty feet of dam he was completely tired out, and after a hundred feet he was moving in a haze, and his mind was a blur. Beyond that he couldn't remember anything afterwards, except that three or four times, near the end of the night, when he thought he was definitely going to die and he'd decided he didn't care, he saw the spirits standing beside him on the dam: the Princess was holding out her right arm to him and smiling, and Theodore was raising a paw in salute. Before Tom could speak, they would be gone; but he would feel life flowing in his body again, and he'd keep on.

He didn't remember reaching the water level, or know how he escaped the burst of water when the dam broke. He didn't remember walking home. Mary found him sitting and snoring on the front steps in broad daylight. He told her what had happened, and she said he'd probably caught a touch of fever from the cold water. He might have thought the same himself, except that his hands were blistered and stained with tree pitch, and his boots were half full of golden sand.

He never told stories about himself after that. His strength that could carry two cows was gone. What he could shove and drag and hoist on the farm was no more than what most of his neighbors on the Cannonball could do, and some of them, such as Mary's cousin Febold Feboldsson, could outlift and outhaul him — but that's not part of this story. People asked Tom sometimes about the tales they'd heard about him, both the true ones and the false. But all he'd say in answer, if he said anything at all, was that he'd used up all his spare strength to clear the river one night long ago.

I used to wade down into the current with Tom sometimes, in the spring after a rain, to help him clear stumps and fallen branches from the stream. I asked him once if he'd ever found out what the river was saying. He looked at the flowing water, seeming to listen again, and for a while I thought he wasn't going to answer. But then he said: "What it says is what it does, and nothing more. I believe that's why it lives forever."

Tom Digs
for Silver

When people asked Tom if he ever wished for his old strength back again, he'd always say he didn't. "Too much strength was too much trouble," he'd add, if he was feeling talkative. I believe he really was grateful it was gone, too, for the most part. But I happen to know there was one circumstance that made him wish he was strong again — stronger, that is, than his wife's cousin Febold, who took over the Feboldsson farm across the river after old Njal passed on.

It wasn't usual for Tom to be jealous of his neighbors, but he was jealous of Febold. I'm not saying Febold's land was any better than Tom's land, and I don't want you to think that Febold's thoughts were as clever as Tom's thoughts. Febold was larger, though. His ox, his ox cart, his scythe, his back, and his shoulders — everything about him was half again the size of what Tom had. Febold rarely paid visits to other people's houses, because he had to duck his head and step sideways to get through their doors, and then there wouldn't be a chair large enough for him to sit in. That's the kind of man he was, and it made Tom mad.

Now spring wheat was the crop all down that valley, and before he lost his strength, Tom had always been the first to finish the work with the wheat at every step: with the plowing, the planting, the reaping, the threshing, and the carting of the harvest to the grain bins in Elgin for sale to the cooperative. And now Febold was first. Every year Tom got busy perfecting one or another method to get past Febold in the farm work, but he always ended up losing ground instead, because Febold would copy what Tom had invented.

One bright fall, for example, Tom taught himself to mow wheat with a scythe in each hand. Febold just stared across the river at Tom for a moment, tugged at the waist of his blue coveralls, scratched his yellow hair underneath his red woolen cap, disappeared into his barn, and stomped back out again with three scythes. He mowed with the third by swinging it from between his teeth. Mary would sometimes mention that, as cook in the house, she might be qualified to say that the flapjacks tasted every bit as good for having come out of wheat that was brought in a week later than Febold Feboldsson's wheat. But it only made Tom grumpy. "It was only five days later last year, and this year it's like to be ten," he'd say.

One winter evening — it might have been in '02 or '03 — Tom read in the newsletter the Grange sends out that steam-powered tractors were being manufactured in Minneapolis. "Twenty times as fast as the fastest ox" was what the advertisement said. Tom took out half his savings from the Grant County Bank and stole out of the valley in the middle of the night. He drove his new tractor home in the middle of the night, too, and hid it in his barn so that Febold wouldn't see it.

The next morning, Tom felled half a dozen cottonwood trees along the riverbank. He was going to need logs to feed the tractor's boilers come plowing time. Mary, shaking her head, watched him from the doorstep, and Cousin Febold, scratching his hair under his red woolen cap, watched him from his woodpile on the other side of the river. "If I've heard you say once," Mary chided when he was done, "I've heard you say a hundred times that the Cannonball Valley has the finest trees this side of the Black Hills." But Tom wasn't about to listen. "Don't bother yourself about the trees," he told her. "Just hope Febold won't guess what's afoot." Tom needn't have worried about Febold's guesses, though, since Febold didn't know there could be such a thing as a steam-powered tractor. He wasn't a reading man.

That spring, Febold's big square jaw fell open when Tom drove his tractor out of his barn. Febold sat down on his ox and stared across the river as the tractor roared and wheezed and coughed black smoke and belched white steam into the blue sky. Whooping and laughing, Tom jolted down the furrows at seven miles an hour. After a few minutes, Febold jumped up and shouldered his ox and ran with his plow. Then he put the ox down and hitched his plow to himself. Tom had been dreading for years that Febold would think of that. But this year he didn't care. His fields were all plowed in two days, and Febold didn't finish his till a week had gone by.

I have to tell you, though, that Tom didn't bring his wheat in sooner than Febold that year. Tom knew that Febold must have ridden off to Bismarck for his own steam tractor, considering the number of tall and stately cottonwood trees that Febold was felling on his side of the riverbank. But he never guessed that, come harvest time, Febold would roar out of his barn with a steam-powered threshing machine bumping along behind his tractor. Some fast-talker in Bismarck must have sold it to him. Tom's threshing machine was powered by his mules. His seven-day start was lost in a single afternoon.

Tom didn't read any Grange newsletters that winter, or any farm equipment catalogues either. Once he'd gone to buy a steam-powered thresher for himself, he hadn't the savings left for anything else. He took to spending long nights on the Cannonball River, wading and splashing and worrying his way far up the current. He tried to convince himself that Mary was right, that bringing in the harvest behind Febold or ahead of Febold didn't count for anything at all. But he couldn't get himself to believe it. Just once, he told himself; if he could be first just once, then maybe he wouldn't care any more, and Febold could go ahead and be number one for the rest of their lives. But no matter how far up the river he waded, no plan came into his mind.

One cold night in March, as Tom was stepping down from his fields and breaking through the glittering shelves of thin ice along the riverbank on his way into the current, his glance fell on a bright stone lying beneath the water. He thought he'd noticed it on other nights that winter, too, when the moon shone straight down into the river. The water had always been shaded in other years, before he and Febold had cut down the tallest trees along the banks. Tom stared at the bright stone. It seemed to be the color of silver — although that might have been a trick of the moonlight. Suddenly he wanted to bring it out of the river and touch it. He waded out and reached down into the frigid water. But the stone was set too deep in the riverbed for him to move.

With his hands and booted feet, and then with a shovel he fetched down from his barn, Tom cleared away the mud and gravel from around the silver stone, only to find that it wasn't just a stone, but a boulder, and not just a boulder but a deep-set ridge that ran for ten, twenty, thirty feet and more straight down the center of the riverbed. With a mattock he chipped away a diamond-shaped sheet of it and held it up smooth and shining in the moonlight. It looked every bit like he had found a vein of true silver beneath the gravel bottom of the Cannonball.

Tom washed the diamond-shaped sheet in the current, dried it on his sleeve, and put it under his coat. Then he shoveled gravel back over the vein and hoped the flow of water would wash away his diggings so that Febold wouldn't spy it in the morning.

Tom read the agricultural machinery catalogues all the way into the village the next day; his horse knew the road, so he didn't need to watch where he was going. He called on Mr. Albrechtberger, who sold jewelry and clocks in a corner of his general store, for a talk about a certain diamond-shaped sheet of metal. Then he walked whistling across the street to the Grant County Bank for a pleasant talk with the vice president about the trading price of silver.

That night Tom stole back out into the river to clear away the gravel from around the silver ridge beneath the water. He multiplied dollars and calculated victory as he dug. Five sheets of silver would buy him a gasoline-powered truck. A gasoline-powered truck could haul his harvest to the grain bins in Elgin in four round-trips in a single long day. Febold, in his ox cart, would need four days. Tom would have gained three days right at the end of the harvest, too late for Febold to catch up with him, the way he'd always caught up before. That one year, Tom would be first. If Febold bought himself a truck to haul his grain the next year, what would it matter? Tom had already promised himself that one year of victory would be enough.

But the more Tom dug and thought, and chipped and planned, the less happy he was about just one year. He didn't want Febold to win the next year, either, or the year after that. Febold had always won. Now it should be Tom's turn to always win.

Tom put down his mattock and looked at his diggings. Not just five sheets of silver, but fifteen sheets shimmered in the moonlight. Fifteen sheets of silver would buy him a steam shovel as well as a truck, and with a steam shovel he could dam up the current, dry up the riverbed, dig deep into the mud and gravel, and yank the entire vein of silver out of the earth. He would be rich, richer than Febold, richer than the general-store owner and the bank vice president and anyone else in the valley. He could buy a second tractor and hire a man to drive it. He could buy anything.

The fifteen sheets that Tom had chipped from the spine of the silver ridge had all broken off in the same diamond shape, as if he had flaked off a great fish's scales. It was true that, by rights, half the silver sheets belonged to Febold, since the ridge ran right along the center of the riverbed. Tom hadn't actually forgotten about that. But he put the thought away from his mind. "When a man has an idea the size of the idea I had in my head, there isn't room in there for much of anything else," is how he explained it to Mary afterwards.

Tom drove his new steam shovel home from Bismarck in the dark of a rainy night. For two stormy days he felled trees and split wood to burn in the boiler. On the third afternoon, when the round sun came out glaring from behind the black clouds, Tom rode his steam shovel down into the current to start ripping up the riverbed to tear out the silver. It didn't surprise him much when Febold came hurrying out of his house, still buttoning his suspenders, because the clanking and roaring of that steam shovel might have been enough to raise the sleepers in the churchyard ten miles down the valley. What did surprise Tom was to see Febold race back to his barn and in five minutes come roaring and clanking across his fields to the river in his own steam shovel.

Febold stopped at the riverbank, stood up on the driver's seat, and waved his red woolen cap over his head. "Need some help there, Cousin?" he bellowed above the din.

Tom put his steam shovel on idle, set his straw hat back on his head, thought a while, and said, "I figured you'd be driving one of these steam shovels by about now, Febold."

"Yep," said Febold. "Soon as Mr. Schmitz sent word you'd been buying again, I got myself on over there. Bought it on time, is what they call it." Schmitz was the dealer in machinery in Bismarck. Tom had sworn the man to a promise not to tell Febold about steam shovels, but maybe the man had forgotten.

Tom and Febold looked at each other for a time, each from the top of his steam shovel. Febold revved his engine once or twice, and mushrooms of smoke and soot popped from his smokestack into the air. It was clear to Tom that his cousin had no idea what a steam shovel was for, or why Tom had bought one. He was waiting to see what Tom would do so he could copy it. Tom, meanwhile, was searching his brain for something believable the two of them might do with the steam shovels, instead of digging for silver.

As Tom thought, his idle eye fell upon a swirl of muddy water trapped beside a stump on Febold's side of the river. When Febold had felled that tree for his tractor's boilers, his ox team must have ripped the stump out from its moorings, and the stump had capsized into the river with its root-ball in the air. The swirling current was deepening the wound in the bank.

"See the way that stump is making an eddy in the current?" Tom said suddenly, pointing with his hat.

"I see it," said Febold, looking at it.

"Ever think how that eddy's going to wash away more of your bank there, Cousin?"

"Never thought how it would," Febold said.

Tom hadn't thought about it before, either, but he didn't say so. "All that tree-falling we done kind of weakened the bank and silted things up some, I'd have to say," Tom said. "The water ain't as clear as it's accustomed."

"No, I don't guess it may be," said Febold, gazing around doubtfully.

"And see on my side, all them dead branches spread-eagled in the water so they catch the dead leaves? We got snags, Cousin, not to speak of silt and eddies and potholes. We're going to end up with our own little Big Muddy here, if we don't clear the stream and straighten out the banks — which is why I got this new machine. Can't say as two were definitely needed."

"You straighten up your side, Cousin, and I'll patch up mine. *Heeee-ap!*" Febold whooped, as he hurtled his machine down the bank into the river. The bank crumpled under the treads, and the steam shovel rocked sideways till it almost tipped over. Turning his machine around, Febold backed it into the center of the river, jerked the bucket high into the air, and swooped it down again so that its teeth plunged into the bank. Earth and stones slid into the water. Billows of mud bloomed in the current around the treads.

"You want to straighten that bank, not carve it up more, Cousin," Tom called out mildly.

"Right," Febold called back, but the bucket of his shovel, loaded with mud and stones, interrupted him by suddenly soaring into the air. Clods of mud flew out from the raised bucket and thudded down on Tom's machine or splashed into the river. Febold leaned squinting over the levers and dials in front of him. "That there Schmitz feller gave me a lesson, but I guess I disremember some," he said.

Shielding his head with his arms, Tom climbed down from his shovel. Febold's tearing up the bank had made him nervous; he himself had been planning to be a little more delicate with the river. He had an unsettling notion that he'd gone too far again, and that Theodore and the River Spirit, or heaven knew who else, might soon come scold him about it. The excuse he'd just invented for buying a steam shovel — that the river needed repairs — was all too uncomfortably true. His clear, singing river was already choking on stumps and mud, and the steam shovels were tearing at its throat. Not only that, but the treads of Febold's machine were probably grinding into the silver ridge and mangling the silver scales.

Tom waded cautiously across the current towards Febold's steam shovel. They had to get the machines out of the water — that was certain. He was looking anxiously up at Febold's bucket, in case it might be ready to shower more stones on him, when he suddenly felt the silver ridge shake a little beneath him. At first he thought Febold must be rocking his steam shovel on its treads, but Febold was frowning at the pictures in his instruction book. Then, with a jerk, Tom was thrown off his feet and onto his knees. Beneath him the riverbed was heaving and pitching, as if it were a blanket and some giant waking up were trying to fling it off.

Soaked to the waist, Tom stood up and stumbled towards Febold, wondering fearfully if this was what people meant when they talked about earthquakes. The silver ridge lurched upwards and shook like a wet bear as it threw off the mud and stones of the river bottom. Tom grabbed hold of the ladder to Febold's seat. Then the silver ridge arched up beneath the men and the steam shovels, and burst straight up out of the river. It lifted into the air and rose ten, twenty, thirty feet above the water, carrying with it Febold and Tom, stranded and bellowing together on Febold's steam shovel.

Tom opened his eyes after a minute. There, thirty feet below him, were his fields and the roof of his barn, and Mary standing by the door to the corncrib, looking up with shaded eyes. She said afterwards that he lost his grip on the ladder of Febold's steam shovel and came within a whisker of falling off when he saw what the silver ridge actually was. But Tom denied it. "I was kind of expecting that something unexpected might come along; and besides, I'm always interested to make a new acquaintance, provided he keeps a civil tongue," is the way he told it.

Just next to Tom and beneath him, from the side of the long silver hill, a silver leg was hanging, with a golden claw on its end. Tom could see another leg dangling from the other side, too. Looking back past Febold, who sat on his steam shovel with his chest heaving and his red woolen cap pulled down over his eyes, Tom saw two great golden wings gently beating the air.

The wings were made not of feathers but of bare golden skin stretched over spidery bones.

The long, round body, which tapered to a pointed tail, was all clothed in round silver scales. A row of them, diamond shaped, stood upright along the spine. There were gaps in that row, and with a chill Tom counted those gaps: eight, ten, twelve, fifteen scales were missing, the very number that Tom had chipped away from the riverbed with his mattock.

Tom closed his eyes again, hoping that when he opened them he would find himself in the cow shed or maybe in bed. He waited as long as he dared. When he opened his eyes, an enormous head at the end of the silver body had turned around to look at him. Several hundred sharp white teeth lined the long jaw, and two green antlers curved back from the wide forehead. Deep in the dark centers of the great green round eyes burned an orange flame. There was no disputing it now: the head was a dragon's head, and the silver ridge was the dragon's body. Tom remembered Wheatberry telling him that a dragon slept hidden somewhere in the valley, and that no one but the River Spirit dared to wake him.

With a quick twist of his right foreleg, the dragon plucked Febold from his steam shovel and held him in the curve of a single golden talon. Then he plucked Tom off his back with a talon of his left foreleg. The dragon shook himself a little, and Febold's steam shovel slid off his back, plunged down to the riverbed, and crumpled in the mud. The dragon brought the two men up near his face. He said in a rumbling voice that made the men's ears vibrate: "Kindly take off your hats so I can have a better look at you."

Febold had been sputtering since his steam shovel had crashed down below, and now he tore his cap off his face and yelled, "That there was a brand-new machine which cost three hundred seventy-five dollars, and how do you plan to pay for it?"

"We aren't ready for the judgment," the dragon rumbled mildly. "I haven't even begun my investigation. State your names, please, and your places of residence."

"Let me down out of here, confound your tin hide!" Febold yelled. The dragon turned Febold upside down, and Tom noticed the orange flames flickering in the depths of the dragon's eyes.

"Your Honor," Tom said, thinking that "Your Honor" might be the diplomatic way to address a dragon, especially a silver dragon that had just been called tin, "Tom Terry's the name, Your Honor, and this here is my wife's cousin Febold Feboldsson, who's maybe feeling a little testy because that steam shovel was kind of new, or maybe because it's getting close to lunchtime. We farm this valley of ours, and we hope you'll accept our apologies for waking you up. It wasn't intentional."

"You farm this valley of *yours?*" the dragon said, raising one eyebrow that curled towards his antlers.

Tom bowed in reply as best he could, considering that his legs were dangling thirty feet above the ground and a dragon's talon was clamped around his waist.

The dragon didn't seem to notice. He was studying a large gold chronometer on his wrist. On it were several dials with symbols Tom had never seen before. A gust of a sigh hissed out from between the dragon's teeth. "It seems this nap has gone on just too long," he said. "I've neglected the problem of you humans."

Tom had been considering how to talk his way back to solid ground. "It's actually very simple, Your Honor," he began. "If you're wondering why we've been working those steam shovels in the river . . ."

"First things first," the dragon interrupted. "Perhaps you would tell me why you stole fifteen scales from my spine?"

Tom cleared his throat. "Yes, well, that, you see, that was just to buy the steam shovels, the reason for which, like I was trying to tell you . . ."

"Each thing in its place," the dragon said, interrupting again. "Do you often steal when you want something, or was this a special case?"

"A special case, a special case, believe me, Your Honor," Tom said. "If I'd only known the silver belonged to you, why, naturally I wouldn't have taken it."

"Whom did you think the silver belonged to?" the dragon asked.

"You knew it was half mine, and I'll have your hide for it, Cousin," Febold shouted, having suddenly understood something he hadn't understood before, perhaps because the blood was rushing to his head as he dangled up-side down.

The dragon turned him right side up and peered at him a minute. "And just how did the silver become half yours?"

"Because it was in the middle of the river," Febold yelled, glaring with red face and popping eyes across the dragon's nose at Tom.

"Let me have this right," the dragon said, in a voice that hinted at a limit to his patience. "Half the river is yours, and the other half belongs to your cousin?"

"That's the case, Your Honor," Tom said hastily. He was wishing that Febold would leave the talking to somebody else, namely himself.

"And how did the river come to belong to you?" the dragon asked, raising his voice and fixing upon Tom again the gaze of his round eyes, which were filling up with the orange fire.

Tom tried pretending he was standing on the ground with his legs set wide apart, in order to give himself some confidence, but the air beneath him didn't give him proper support. He wanted to hook his thumbs in his suspenders and snap them, but the dragon's claw had pinned his suspenders to his chest. "Well sir, Your Honor," he said, "the valley was empty and open for the taking when our people came. It's true the Indians were here on occasion, but my pa bought his place fair and square from the railroad for two dollars and fifty cents an acre, and so did Febold's Uncle Njal, and I'm right sorry about your scales," Tom finished, rather lamely, he thought.

"You're willing to be sorry about my scales, since you've already been to the bank to cash them in," the dragon remarked. His voice was growing a little louder.

"Right, right, and I *am* sorry about it," Tom said. "But if the river was yours for your bed, I think you really should have told somebody, if I could make a suggestion."

"I never said the river was mine," the dragon said, quite loudly now.

"Then whose is it?" Tom asked, but he wished, not for the first time in his life, that he could learn when to stop talking.

"How could you not know whose it is? How could you think it was only yours?" the dragon demanded in a roar that made Tom's ears ache. He brought Tom up a few feet from one of his burning eyes. Without intending it, Tom stared into the flames. They seemed to be moving closer and closer towards him. He shook and sweated in the golden claw. He wanted to look away, but the dragon's gaze held him. He opened his mouth to speak, but he couldn't find his voice.

After a long minute, the dragon's hissing sigh suddenly burst out from between his rows of teeth. "No one objects to your just *using* things," he said more quietly, "but you humans make such an enormous mess for your size of creature. It's getting these days so that no one wants to live anywhere near you. But perhaps you don't care." He looked below him sadly at the rubble of stumps and stones and sodden branches along the riverbank. "Have you thought of how you're going to manage if you drive away everyone else but yourselves? You haven't," the dragon concluded.

The burning eyes released him, and Tom looked down towards the river below. Finding his voice, he said, "Febold's machine is wrecked, Your Honor, but we still have my steam shovel, and I'd say we could probably put the river back to rights soon enough."

"You've botched something with one of your machines, and now you think another machine will be enough to set it right, is that it?" the dragon said, but in a milder tone, as if pity, maybe, had conquered his disgust.

"Well, there'll be some handwork in the cleanup," Tom began.

But the dragon cut him off. "You can talk cleverly, but you can't think sensibly. A pity." He snorted faintly, and a small puff of smoke popped from each of his nostrils. He moved Tom away from his face. His examination was done. The flames sank back into the depths of his eyes. "As for you" — the dragon brought Febold up near his right eye for a moment, and then moved him away again — "you have strength, but you don't know what it's for."

Suddenly the men noticed that the dragon was floating slowly towards the earth. "As it is," he said, in the soft rumble of distant summer thunder that his voice had been when he'd first spoken to them, "I'm afraid I'll have to leave. I can't sleep in such a rumpled bed as this. Fortunately for you, the River Spirit has told me about one of you, and actually put in a good word for you. She said there's more to you than meets the eye" — here his right eye regarded Tom briefly — "which I find scarcely believable, but since the Princess said it, I can't doubt it. Therefore, I'll be taking thought to your welfare in my absence."

Tom and Febold watched nervously as the fields rushed up towards them. "Go easy on the landing, will you?" said Febold in a quavering voice. Ten feet above the ground, the dragon let go of them, and they plummeted into the mud of the riverbank. Tom rolled over and looked up: standing beside them, the dragon was now no more than twelve feet long. He had transformed himself as they fell. His golden wings were folded on his shoulders.

He watched the men stand up. "No broken bones?" he asked. "An acceptable landing? This way, then, if you'd like to follow me to my hall. It's not far." Unfolding his wings again and tucking his legs up against his body, the dragon flew silently along the bank.

Tom stared after him only for a moment; then he stumbled along behind him among the roots and stones. Febold called out, "Hey, Cousin, come back here! Are you gone crazy?" But Tom kept walking after the dragon. Even before he had mentioned the River Spirit, Tom had suspected the dragon might be peaceable, and probably even friendly, if you didn't irritate his temper. Now that he had invited them to his hall, Tom had no intention of missing his chance. "Febold didn't have any experience with these sorts of folks, so you've got to excuse him for being a little suspicious," Tom said to Mary afterwards — rather generously, she thought.

Up ahead, the dragon was hovering above the water. Reaching down through the current, he was pushing mud and gravel aside to clear a space in the riverbed. As Tom walked up, he saw through the water a pair of silver doors that lay flush with the bottom of the river. He wondered how many times he had tramped over them in the past without knowing it. He could see now that an image of the River Spirit's spring was carved on each door, and above it was the image of a pearl, with golden lines flowing out of it, as if to represent light. With a silver key on a chain that he had drawn from around his neck, the dragon reached through the water again and opened the doors upwards. The doors shoved the current to each side. A corridor, now open to the air, led down beneath the riverbed. "Come in," the dragon said, turning around to the men.

"That ain't anyplace we're going into," said Febold, who had stomped up behind them. "We're going on home."

"No," said Tom, as he looked past the dragon and down the corridor, which shone faintly with a silver glow. "If I can, Your Honor, I'd be pleased to go along for a look."

"Each as he wishes," the dragon said, adding to Febold, "Perhaps your cousin will share with you, if you don't come."

"Share? What's this, now? Share what? Is this about money?" Febold said sharply.

"You can follow me," the dragon said, and he flew through the doors. Tom followed quickly, and he heard Febold's boots thumping in after.

The corridor sloped gradually downwards. The silver floor was smooth and even, and the straight walls felt cool to the touch of Tom's fingers. Light flickered from the silver ceiling, though Tom could see no source of it; there were no flames. All was silence but for the fall of the men's boots and the faint swish of the dragon's wings. At last the corridor came to an end before a second pair of silver doors, each carved with the images of the spring and the pearl.

"You will have to pardon the simplicity of my hall," the dragon said as he stopped and drew the key from around his neck again. "It's not often that I welcome any visitors here, and it's been a very long time since I've had any need of a palace."

He opened the doors inwards and floated through them into a long room. Like the corridor, it was lit from the ceiling by invisible fires. On the silver floor, and between two rows of round columns, thin straight lines of inlaid gold led down the hall. They glowed faintly from a light within. At the far end of the hall, the lines flowed together, then curved outwards again to form the spray of a fountain.

Beyond were two stairs leading to a platform, and on it stood a couch without a back. Its scrolled ends were set about with swirls of blue gems. Tom recognized them: they were the same, only smaller, as the gem that had flashed in the night from the River Spirit's forehead. Near the left end of the dragon's couch, just at the place, Tom thought, where a reclining dragon might be want-ing a pillow, lay a flattened pile of diamonds. A large green pearl, which Tom recognized from the image on the doors, was floating in the air by itself above the diamonds.

The dragon glided up the steps. Unfolding his legs, he stood beside the couch. Febold stopped halfway down the hall and clasped Tom's shoulder. "Better stay back here, Cousin. You don't know what he's planning." But Tom walked on. He took off his straw hat and held it in his hands.

"I'm trying to think how you're going to carry them," the dragon said, as Tom stood below him at the base of the platform. "We should have brought along a basket of some sort." As he spoke, he stood up slightly on his back legs, plunged his clawed hands into the pillow of diamonds, gathered up two hand-fuls, and held them out to Tom. "Do you have any room in your pockets?"

Tom found that he'd lost his voice again, but he shook his head. It wasn't that the pockets of his overalls were full; in fact, there was nothing in them but his handkerchief. "But I already owed him for his scales," he told Mary afterwards, "and I'd torn up his front yard. It didn't seem right."

"Take them," the dragon said, holding out the diamonds. "You will need them."

Febold was thumping down the hall, calling out, "Take them if he's dumb enough to give them, Cousin. Don't he owe us for that steam shovel?"

"He's right that you should take them," the dragon said, "but for the wrong reasons."

"Won't you want them, though?" Tom said. "A dragon needs a pillow, seems to me, same as a man does."

"I won't need them here," said the dragon. "I've already told you I'll be going."

"Looks like that'll be a good thing for us," Febold remarked, as he stood beside Tom, his hands stretched out, palms up.

"You are mistaken," the dragon replied. He turned to Tom, saying, "Take them, friend, and use them well."

Tom stood on the first step of the platform, and the dragon tipped the diamonds into his hands. Tom turned and let half of the stones fall into Febold's grasp, then put the rest in his right front pocket. The dragon gathered up two more handfuls from the pillow, and these, too, he gave to Tom, who again handed half to Febold before putting the rest in his left front pocket. The dragon returned to the pillow four times more, for twelve handfuls in all, until not a diamond was left on his couch, and the men's pockets were so heavy with gems that their suspenders sagged.

"What about that one there?" Febold said, pointing to the sea-green pearl that shone alone now above the couch.

"That's nothing for us," Tom said sharply.

"Why not?" Febold said. "He gave us all the rest of it."

The dragon walked down off the platform, saying to Febold, "It's my wishing-pearl. Good dragons have them, if they are lucky. You might say they are our pets. But you may try to take it, if that will satisfy you."

Febold looked around for a moment, maybe wondering if he dared climb the steps. Then, in two strides, he ran up onto the platform and swept his hand around to snatch the pearl. Just at that moment, the pearl floated farther up into the air, beyond his reach. Febold jumped up after it, but he couldn't jump very high, because of the weight of the diamonds in his pockets. The pearl sailed slowly over to the dragon, who said, "That's settled, then. We can go."

The dragon folded in his legs. With the pearl bobbing and floating in little loops on ahead of him, he flew down the hall. The glow faded from the golden lines in the floor as he passed over them. The light from the ceiling grew dim. The two men followed the dragon out of the hall and up the silver corridor, where the hidden lights went out behind them.

Outside on the riverbank, evening had fallen. The men stood on the bank as the dragon took the key from his neck and locked the doors. Without a word, he rose into the air. Suddenly he was a hundred feet long again above them. Beating his golden wings, with the pearl floating and faintly shining before him, he glided along the valley and disappeared beyond the hills into the dark blue sky of the spring night.

The next day, Febold rode off to Bismarck to sell some of his diamonds. He bought a new steam shovel to replace the one the dragon had shrugged off into the mud, and he also made his missus the first farmlady in southwestern North Dakota to own a private automobile. Before going home, he paid a visit to a dentist to have gold caps fitted to two of his front teeth. He'd broken them the night before by chomping down hard on one of the dragon's diamonds, to test if they were real.

"They're genuine, though — first water is what they call it — and they fetch something considerable at the jeweler's, Cousin," was his advice to Tom when he stopped by later to show off the automobile.

Tom went to Bismarck, too, riding on his steam shovel. He sold it back to the dealer. He sold his steam tractor and his steam-powered thresher, too, as part of the bargain. He pleased Mary by telling her that he and steam power had had a parting of the ways. He said he couldn't see cutting down any more cottonwood trees beside the river to fire the boilers.

"The dragon said we make too much of a mess," Tom told her. "You should have seen that eye-fire of his when he asked what makes us human beings think the river belongs to us. Just to remember it makes me sweat."

Some of the money he made from selling the machines Tom spent on cottonwood saplings, which he planted along the riverbank. But he didn't sell his diamonds. He stored them in a cardboard box on a top shelf in the kitchen. "The dragon said I'm to use them well," he told his missus, "and I'll have to wait till I know what he meant by it."

That spring, no rain came to the Cannonball Valley. The farmers hitched up their mules and carried water in barrels from the river to the fields to keep the seedlings from shriveling in the soil. No rain fell that summer, either. Day after day, the sun shone in a hot and empty sky. The harvest in August was one-tenth the size of the harvest in an ordinary year. The farmers plowed the fields and waited for winter to cover the land with snow. But no snow fell. People half across the state were shaking their heads over the strange drought in the Cannonball Valley. On the prairie, and in the other hills and valleys, the winter was no different than it ever was.

When he wasn't carrying water from the river to dampen down the soil, Tom stood by his barn and gazed at the horizon. He was waiting for the heads of black clouds to rise and look back at him from over the hills; but he was also waiting for the dragon. He couldn't give an explanation to Mary, because he couldn't explain it to himself. "I expect the drought is here because he isn't," was the best he could do with it.

Mary didn't argue with him. She'd also seen the dragon, although not at close quarters as Tom had, and she reckoned that if a dragon was possible, anything was. She looked her husband in the eye and asked him just what he was planning to do about it, since he was the one who'd dared to steal the dragon's scales and drive him from his sleep beneath the river.

Tom figured she was right, and he took down some diamonds from the kitchen shelf. He cashed them in at the state bank in Bismarck, and rode the railroad east to the Red River Valley, where no one knew him, to buy wheat out of storage. He had the wheat delivered to the cooperative in Elgin and sold, and had the profits given to his neighbors in the Cannonball Valley. That way, Tom told himself, no one would go bankrupt, at least, because of his mistake.

All through the next spring, the sun shone over the Cannonball from a cold and empty sky. Tom paid calls on the farmers to persuade them to dig wells by the river. "We could be in for another dry year," he said. But after a second summer without rain, the wells ran dry. Soon the river itself was no more than a thread of a current that wound down the riverbed among the muddy stones. There was no harvest that year. Again Tom cashed in some diamonds, and again the farmers on the Cannonball were paid by the cooperative for wheat they hadn't grown. The farmers were grateful, but they didn't like the mystery. Some of them said the Cannonball was cursed, and they sold their farms to Febold for half what they were worth and moved to California.

The next spring, the third spring of the drought, Tom and some of his neighbors built dams and reservoirs in the hills on either side of the valley, where there were still a few live streams. Tom brought in iron pipe, and they laid it down to the valley floor, so that at least there would be water for the people and the animals to drink. No water ran in the river; the mud dried hard on the stony bottom. There came a silence to the valley that the farmers had never known before. When there was wind, dry dust from the fields whirled in the air.

All Tom had left now from the dragon's pillow was a single diamond, the largest and most beautiful of all that the dragon had given him. If he held it up just right to the sun, he thought he could see a sea-green light floating and flashing like a dragon's pearl in its depths. He had a secret wish to keep that diamond for himself. He thought that maybe, once the drought was over, he could use the diamond to buy some machine, a miraculous, as yet uninvented machine that would burn no trees and leave the river clear, and the air bright, and the earth unscarred, and yet would let him bring in the harvest before Febold just one time.

He often paced half the night up and down the dry bed of the Cannonball, clutching that last diamond in his fist so tightly that its facets cut his hands. But at last one morning, he buckled it into his wallet and rode off to Bismarck to cash it in. "Don't ask me where this came from," he said as he gave the money out evenly to the farmers of the valley. "It's not mine, and if I told you whose it was, you wouldn't believe me." He walked home with empty hands. "It's done, Mary," he told her when he sat down in the kitchen. "They're all spent."

On the first night of June, not long before sunrise, rain came to the Cannonball Valley. No one had seen the clouds coming. The day before, the sky had been its usual endless blue. But rain was what was drumming on the farmhouse roofs, and rain was what was clattering on the cow sheds and the barns. The men and women and the children of the farms ran out of their houses in their nightclothes to turn up their faces and hands to the falling water. All the next day the rain fell, and all the day after. The farmers walked around in their fields, with their straw hats streaming, just to plunge their hands into moist soil and to cake their boots with mud. On the third night, about an hour after midnight, a rumble of thunder like a dragon's roar swept across the valley, and suddenly the people in their beds heard a sound they had almost forgotten: the rushing of water in the river.

I've already told you that Tom sold his steam-powered machinery. He didn't replace it, and he never owned a gasoline-powered automobile, either, or anything else that made his life move faster than he thought it ought to go. It seemed that the more machines his neighbors bought for their houses and their farms — especially his rich neighbor Febold — the fewer things Tom owned, so that there was almost nothing in his house and barn when he was old, except some furniture and tools and peace. "He'll tell you he's rich," he said once about Febold, "but he isn't. He'd tell you he'd guess he was happy, too, if you asked him. But every day he's still running around like a starved chicken in a hurry to get something he doesn't have. Now what kind of rich and happy is that?"

I'd often go down to the river in those days, to find Tom standing in the moonlight with the current rushing past him. But sometimes he'd be no-where in sight, though I was certain I'd spied him wading into the river. I asked him once if the dragon had come back, and if he ever went to see him in his hall. He didn't answer. I hadn't actually expected him to.

Tom Goes to the Bearback Races

One May evening, when Tom was in his later years, he hurried himself up out of sleep on account of not liking the dream he was in: someone was driving a bulldozer over his chest. He opened his eyes to find Theodore staring at him. The tree spirit was squatting on Tom's stomach and thumping on Tom's chest with his right hind foot.

"So!" Theodore said, crossing his rabbit arms. "If it weren't for the Princess, you'd have a death to make excuses for. Jack Pine's people were ready to take revenge on your new house, too, if the Princess hadn't forbidden it. And here you are, sleeping in your bed without the faintest idea about any of it."

"The Princess? What revenge? Who's Jack Pine?" Tom said, shaking sleep out of his brains and taking off his nightcap.

"Your blockhead of a son," Theodore scolded, "shot a bear this afternoon, up on the hill in the woods where you're building that ridiculous retirement house of yours. And of all bears, it had to be Jack Pine's bear. The Princess was kind enough to heal the poor animal in order to keep the peace — luckily for you."

Tom pinched his earlobe to make sure he was awake before he started in defending himself. He already knew that his son Orville had spied a pack of bears prowling around the foundation of the new house, and that Orville had shot one of them to drive them away.

"Master Theodore, sir," Tom began, "I'm real glad to see you, and my respects to the Princess" — here Tom wanted to nod for the sake of politeness, except a man can't manage a polite-looking nod when he's lying on his back with a tree spirit on his stomach — "but I don't believe I know a Jack Pine. The only Jack in this valley is Jack Gustafson down at the feed store. Now he keeps chickens and a brand-new nineteen-forty-six Chevrolet in his barn, but he don't keep any bears that I ever heard about. So I can't see as I'm beholden to any of your Jacks," Tom finished, a bit more testily than maybe he had meant to.

"Keep your voice down, sir, or you'll wake up your family," Theodore said sternly, with a firm thump to Tom's chest.

"You'll have to pardon me," Tom apologized, wishing Theodore would ease off of him so he could breathe better, "but I got a spot of rheumatism, which makes me aggravated. Now I grant you my son Orville was a blockhead for downing that bear, same as you say, and in fact I used that very word in telling him as much, so I don't know . . ."

"*Why* you don't know," Theodore interrupted — and Tom decided to stay interrupted, in order to avoid any further rabbit thumps — "*Why* you don't know, at the age of seventy-four, that Jack Pine is the chief of the forestmen in the pine woods on the hill behind your own farm, is entirely beyond me. Why you're building a house smack in the middle of the very clearing where the forestmen run their bear races is even farther beyond me. I've told Jack you'll meet him at the clearing at midnight to discuss this inexcusable state of affairs. And now good night to you." Pushing off from Tom's stomach so that Tom said, "Oof!" Theodore sailed to the floor and kick-walked out of the room, right through the closed door, with his flattened-back ears pointing angrily behind him.

Grumbling into his moustache, Tom pulled on his overalls over a flannel shirt. So as not to wake Orville and Orville's wife, Belinda Jane, and their five children, who were all asleep here and there in the house, Tom walked downstairs to the kitchen in his stocking feet, feeling his way around the steps that had a reputation for squeaking in the dark. I tell you this because I don't want you to think Tom wasn't considerate of his family, or wasn't a thoughtful grandfather who a young person might want to play gin rummy with, if it was raining out. He was — on the days he managed to locate a pleasant mood. On the other days he was likely to snap anyone's head off, if anyone happened to be in the vicinity. He'd feel aggravated even in his sleep. He said it was because he couldn't do so well without Mary, who had died the year before; he said it wasn't fair she'd left him alone, and I don't guess it was.

But if I'm to tell you the truth, which my mother particularly insisted on, I have to say that Tom began having trouble with his temper quite a few years back, long before Mary passed away: in fact, ever since he'd started to feel old. His moustache had turned white without so much as asking his permission; his legs ignored orders and stumbled on the doorstep; his shins turned chilly in his boots when he took a night stroll up the river for an evening think. It didn't please his pride any, either, to have to rely on his son for all the heavy work on the farm. Everything about old age made Tom testy, and some days he didn't care who knew it. It got so Mary would tell him he'd have to move out of the house and live alone in the pine woods until he learned to keep his temper better.

After Mary died, her idea that he should hide his anger in the woods kept building itself in his mind. She hadn't meant it seriously at the time; but what if he did build his own house up on the hill, still on the Terry property and near the family, but not too near? Then, if the grandchildren's bickering pained his ears, or if they camped a tin army in the hallway where a feller had to walk, he could stomp up the hill and teach the squirrels how to properly scold. He could rant at the trees.

That winter, after a few icy nights of thinking up and down the frozen river, he trudged through the snow up the cart track to the woods and found the ideal place for a new house — at least, he thought it was the ideal place: an almost perfectly round, just about perfectly flat clearing among the pines, with possibilities for a fine view of the valley below. As soon as spring thawed the ground, he set to digging the foundation. Orville rented a bulldozer, as he didn't share his father's suspicion of machines, and by May they had the cellar built and the joists nailed down for the first floor. Then — on the day that I'm telling you of — Orville came in to dinner saying he'd downed a bear.

That night, after pulling on his boots, Tom eased the kitchen door open and stepped out into the spring air. He looked at his pocket watch in the flicker of his kerosene lantern: twenty minutes to midnight. Muttering to himself, he yanked his walking stick down from its hook by the door and stumped quickly across the yard. Suddenly a flashlight beam bobbed into the dark from behind the barn, and a voice called out in a loud whisper:

"Grandpa? Are we going up to the new house?"

It was Nick, who was twelve, and Tom's favorite grandchild — which Tom thought he'd kept to himself, although it was obvious to everyone, since Nick was the only person Tom never snapped at.

"*I'm* going up to the new house," Tom said to him, "which I ain't pleased to tell you, and *you're* going back to bed."

"I can't go back to bed, Grandpa." Nick hurried after Tom, who was already toiling up the cart track. "I've gotten too tall for that couch in the kitchen where Ma put me since the twins were born, and I can't sleep sometimes. That's why I heard you on the stairs." His dark brows frowned. "And anyway, you're going to need help up in the woods. Bears are serious business. I've got my rifle."

"No rifle, boy," Tom said. "You'll leave that behind."

"You mean I can come?"

Tom didn't answer. Taking that for "yes," Nick propped the gun against a fence rail and walked on beside his grandfather. Of course, you won't remember Theodore mentioning anything about bringing along a grandson, because he didn't mention it; but, by the same token, he hadn't forbidden it, either. Tom was probably relieved not to have to meet the angry forestmen alone. But I believe he was also thinking of something else. Nick had always been the child who'd pricked up his ears whenever the dinner conversation turned to Tom's negotiations with spirits. Now that Tom was old, he wanted some help with the negotiating. He wanted there to be someone who could speak to the spirits after he was gone. "I always figured Nick had the makings of a diplomat," Tom told me later, "seeing as how he always won his squabbles with his sisters."

So Tom and Nick climbed the hill in silence, until they reached a small, open flat, halfway up the cart track, where the Terry creek tumbled out of the woods, talking to itself in the dark. Ahead, the hill loomed over them, rising against the sky, blacker than the night. It was covered with old pines. The trees rose in a high wall on the other side of the flat, as if to defend the hill from siege. They stood thick and close together, and their dusty scent was heavy on the air. Their scraggy tops moaned faintly; their jagged branches waved and rustled in the wind.

Tom remarked: "Your pa thinks we maybe ought to move the new house out of the woods and down to this flat here, if the bears are going to be trouble up top. But I'm not about to do it."

"You're right, Grandpa," the boy said. "The house has to be up top."

"Oh, that so? Why might that be?"

"Because of the trees," Nick said. "I know you like the river, but the pine woods are actually the best place on the farm. You and Pa just don't realize it."

"Well, now. I didn't know you ever came up the hill."

"Sometimes I do, especially at night." As he spoke, they followed the track into the woods. Dark trees closed in around them. Black branches groaned and groped at them as they passed. "Hear them creaking all around us, Grandpa? I definitely think they're spooky. See how their twigs are all woven together like in spider webs?" Nick bounced his flashlight among the drooping branches. "What I especially like is to walk in and scare myself — not too much, of course. I make up stories about all that black space in there." His flashlight beam was swallowed by the emptiness between the trees. "It's cold and dark even in the daytime. You have to watch out or the stubs of dead branches will stab you in the eye."

They walked on for a minute without speaking. Suddenly an owl screeched, startling them. A dead limb crashed through branches in the distance. Tom asked after a moment, "What stories do you make up, my boy?"

"Well, nothing special, really, but don't you think there could be some pretty strange things living in the woods?"

"You could be right," Tom said, half to himself. He was thinking he might have had the same opinion when he was Nick's age, except it would have been about the river.

"I could be right? Really?"

"Well, what kind of things do you figure could be living in here?"

"I don't know. That's part of the fun. Any kind of thing you could imagine. Like if you went up to one of these old pines just thinking — not even carrying a chain saw, but I mean just *thinking* — about cutting the tree down, something with hairy arms would probably reach around your chest from behind and pin your arms."

They had reached the clearing at the top of the hill. Pines stood around its edge like soldiers, with their peaked helmets raised rough and black against the stars. On one side only, the hill dropped steeply away, and here the trees stood aside to reveal a view of the valley, which was sleeping in shadow far below. Near the opening, the foundation of Tom's new house lay in the gloom. The rows of white floor joists glimmered in the starlight.

It was midnight on Tom's watch. "Look," he said.

Dark shapes were filing out of the forest: bears. There were ten, twelve, fourteen of them now, at the far edge of the clearing, walking back and forth with their swaying, shambling bear's gait. Then they seemed to line up, in two groups of seven. Suddenly, with a roar, they broke into a run. Throwing their front two feet forward together, then doubling up to bring forward their back feet, they galloped and jostled one another, jaws hanging open, tongues lolling, eyes staring. They hurtled around the edge of the clearing and swerved in a detour around the foundation of the house. Tom and Nick quickly backed up into the shelter of trees as the bears rushed towards them. Their eyes flashed in the light of Tom's lantern.

"I'd definitely say they were racing, if they weren't bears, Grandpa."

"Did you maybe see something on them?" Tom asked.

"On them? What do you mean by 'on them'?"

"Try taking another look, when they come round again."

"What should I be seeing?"

No longer a pack, the bears were spread out now in a speeding circle. As they lumbered past him a second time, Nick gasped. Fur-covered man-shapes were riding on the bears' backs. The men kicked out their long legs and waved their hairy arms around their heads. They shouted with round, open mouths.

Nick stared; then he said: "You knew there'd be spooks here tonight, didn't you."

Tom chuckled to himself, which he'd about forgotten how to do recently. "Nick found his voice again a lot faster than I ever did, on similar occasions," he boasted afterwards to anyone who would listen. To Nick he said, "They ain't spooks, my boy. They're spirits. They're forestmen. They're busy at their bear races, just as you say — I know because I got an appointment."

Now some of the bears seemed to push themselves to a final rush, passing others that had slowed, while a few dropped back to a walk. Then one of the bears suddenly turned into the center of the circle and stopped. Its rider leaped off and jumped up and down. He tipped back his face and whooped. The other bears trotted to a halt.

"I think we got a winner," Tom said.

All the riders dismounted and began milling around the clearing, while the bears sat rolling back on their haunches, panting hoarsely, their chests heaving. One of the forestmen was walking slowly across the clearing towards the foundation. His legs kicked out loosely, and his furry body rolled slightly as he walked, like the bear who followed him. He was thin and very tall, and his long arms dangled to his knees. On his flat, round face were black lips, a black bear's nose, and round eyes dark to their edges.

"That'll be the chief of these folks now, I reckon," Tom whispered. "He's the feller whose bear your pa shot this afternoon. Not a good choice of

a target, though that's not your pa's fault. They ain't too happy about me building a house in their racecourse, either, and I guess they ain't partial to the sound
of a chain saw."

Nick was still staring, but he said, "I think you mean we're in trouble."

"Well, you might say we got a need for diplomacy." They walked over
to the foundation. "Now, remember your Sunday manners, and kindly speak
up if you see me getting too hot under the hat brim."

The chief of the forestmen stopped in front of Tom. In the dark behind him, the other spirits stood silently in a semicircle, waiting.

"Tom Terry's the name, sir," Tom began, thinking to take charge of
the conversation by starting it. "That's my farm down below. Master Theodore
asked me to come meet you, and I'm honored to be doing so."

The forestman stood taller than Tom by more than a foot, and he
stooped like a bending tree as he looked Tom slowly up and down. "I am Jack
Pine," he said finally, in a deep, slow, heavy voice. "I already know who you
are. You don't know who I am. Why not?"

"I've been wrong not to know you, sir," Tom said smoothly. "I reckon
it's because I haven't generally come to the forest up till now, especially at night.
I've looked to the river — no offense meant."

"No offense meant?" Jack repeated. He moved his round face down
close to Tom's. "You have come to our woods. You have taken our trees. You
have dug up our racecourse." Jack's voice rose hollowly like a tree's moan in
the wind, as he pointed his furry finger at the bear beside him: "And you hurt
my bear. You say there's no offense?" Jack shook his head, his voice now
wooden and deep again: "No, old man. You must go back to the river. You

cannot stay here." He stood up straight, and behind him, the other spirits swung their arms and shouted their agreement in a thick roar.

"Well sir," said Tom, swallowing a moment, although he didn't have anything particular to swallow, and eyeing Jack's bear, which was swinging its head back and forth low to the ground, "I'm right sorry your bear was hurt, although a man could say it shouldn't have been sniffing around my house."

"Your house is in our woods," Jack Pine growled.

"Look, Grandpa, it's like you said," Nick interrupted, pointing. "This bear with Mr. Jack must be the same bear Pa shot. It's got the bent ear, and silver hairs on its back, just like Pa described it. Except it's not hurt, and Pa said he'd downed it. It's a spirit, I'll bet."

"No, it's a bear, Nick," said Tom, who was grateful to be interrupted while he could still find his temper. "The River Spirit fixed him up, see, be- cause" — here he spoke loudly, having sighted a likely opening — "because the River Spirit wants the farmers and the forestmen to be peaceful."

"Hah. You know the River Spirit?" Jack said suspiciously. "Do you talk to her?"

"Yes sir, I do. She wants us to make peace. She don't want us to fight." Tom was keeping things short and simple, to fit with what he saw was Jack's style, so as not to make Jack nervous, and maybe his bear nervous. It cramped Tom a bit, though. He always valued a little fancy language during a negoti- ation. Of course, no one could match the Wind Lady when it came to long- winded, many-layered, curlicued conversation, which Tom found out during a debate over the proper course to be taken by a blizzard. But I'm not bringing up that story while I'm occupied with this one.

"You know the River Spirit wants peace?" Jack was saying to Tom. "Then explain why you hurt my bear. Explain why your house is in our clearing."

"Well sir, here's my answer," said Tom, who had just invented it. "When we put this foundation for the house in the clearing here, we didn't know the clearing was yours, and we didn't know what you used it for. So, you could say we were mistaken. On the other hand, it seems to me there ain't many decent places around here for a retirement house, but any flat place can make a racecourse. There's a dandy flat for racing right nearby, halfway down the hillside where the creek comes out, for instance. Or my son Orville, he runs quite a nifty bulldozer when he's minded to — which I ain't saying I necessarily like — but he can rip you out a nice new racetrack in a day or two right through the woods if you want, in any direction you choose. I'll need to trim up some more trees for lumber, anyhow."

The forestmen behind Jack grunted angrily and pushed closer. Jack was shaking his head. "Old man," he said, "this is quick and clever talk. We do not speak clever talk in the woods. We are slower than you humans and spirits by the river. But we know what we know. You have already taken too many trees, and you cannot take any more."

"Lots of trees here, seems to me," Tom said.

"You cannot," Jack repeated, more loudly.

"Now look," said Tom — whose head had heated up again, and who wished he was in the river, so he could douse his face with a hatful of the current — "Look. So far I only cut trees that were crowding out the cart track. There's a lot of cordwood up here, and we ought to be able to share it. I mean

I ain't proposing to saw the whole woods down and plant it every inch to wheat, without so much as a sapling left for shade, the way my wife's cousin Febold cleared his woods across the river. I don't suppose there's much chance for bear racing over *there*, now is there?"

Tom nodded with satisfaction, feeling he'd scored a shrewd point. He wasn't asking the forestmen for much, after all, compared with what Febold had taken. It surprised him, then, when he noticed the forestmen were staring at him in rigid silence. In their round, flat, black eyes, there was fear and sorrow.

Jack said after a minute: "We never speak of the old forest across the river."

"Were there forestmen in Cousin Febold's woods, too, Mr. Jack, before he cut them down?" said Nick, who probably thought it was already past time to interrupt again.

Blinking slowly, Jack looked directly at Nick for the first time but did not answer.

"I don't think he knew, Mr. Jack. I'm sure he didn't know. He wouldn't have been able to see forestmen like you."

Jack leaned forward again, tipped his pointed ears to the front, and widened his black eyes to study Nick at close quarters. "Do you know this big man?" Jack asked, finally.

"Cousin Febold? Well, sure, but . . . what I mean is, I know my *pa* certainly wouldn't have shot your bear today if he'd seen a forestman with it. You should show yourself to people, Mr. Jack, that's what I'm saying, so they'd know."

"We cannot show ourselves," Jack said. "You and the old man are seeing us now with your own magic. Forestmen have magic only with bears." Jack straightened up and looked out beyond the valley towards Febold's empty hills. His words, Tom said afterwards, sounded like the voices of old trees, if trees could talk: dignified, heavy, and sad. "No, boy. We know your cousin couldn't see us. But he saw the bears, and he shot them. He saw the trees, and he killed them all."

"Did the forestmen there cross the river to live with you, then?"

"Well," said Tom loudly, since he had an uncomfortable feeling that the conversation was heading towards the removal of his house, "I'm sure they found some cottonwoods to live in somewhere."

"Forestmen cannot leave their pine woods, old man," Jack said.

"Why not?" said Tom. "You ought to be a mite more flexible, is what I'm saying."

"No. You haven't understood," Jack said. "We cannot."

"Fiddlesticks," said Tom, who always felt irritated by other people's stubbornness, especially when he had the suspicion that he himself was in the wrong. "There's a great world out there, sir. You just got to be more venture-some. That flat down there, where the creek comes out, for instance. You say you couldn't race your bears there? Have you tried, I'd like to know? Have you ever even taken a look at it?"

Jack shook his head again. "The edge of the forest is our boundary. We cannot leave the hill."

"'Cannot,'" Tom snorted, feeling good and aggravated, and wid-ening his stance a notch, "is a word you use too much. You're asking me, I take it, to vacate your premises and find a new site for my house. Am I right?"

Jack nodded slowly. "You must move, old man. We are sorry."

"Well, then," said Tom, "I'm asking you just to take a look at my alternative, see? Take yourselves halfway down the hill and try out the flat. It might make you a superior racecourse, I'm saying, with the creek right there for a drink, convenient to the bears."

Again Jack was shaking his head, making Tom more exasperated than he'd been since last Tuesday, when he'd stumbled and banged his big toe on the hay rake. Nick said hesitantly, "Grandpa, I think maybe . . ." But Tom, ignoring him, reached out to take Jack's wrist, saying firmly, "Come on, then, let me just show you." To his surprise, his lunging hand passed through Jack's arm as if through air. He should have known it would, but he wasn't thinking, and his momentum pitched him forward so that he lost his balance. As he stumbled, Jack's bear snapped out to catch Tom's forearm in its jaws. Tom fell heavily, shouting, wrenching his arm as the bear still held it. Its teeth punched through Tom's skin.

"Let go, bear," Jack ordered, and he pressed his forefinger against its jaw. But growling and tossing its head, the bear held on.

"Pull the cussed thing off of me, will you?" Tom yelled, as he eyed a thread of blood winding down his arm. "Yank its jaws apart!"

Jack was stroking the bear's neck now, to calm it. "He knows you are angry. Stop being angry, and he will let go, I think."

"Stop being angry, with a bear testing its teeth on my arm?" Tom shouted.

"Try, Grandpa," Nick pleaded.

"I can't, dad blast it!" Tom yelled. He had been twisting his arm to free it, but as he did the bear's teeth had only cut deeper. Now he sat back, breathing heavily and shivering with cold sweat. His arm was numb, and his head ached and felt strange. He was ashamed in front of Nick, and afraid of bleeding to death among these thick-headed bear handlers, and most of all, mad that he didn't know how to stop being mad. "I can't," he muttered to himself.

Nick was biting his lip and gripping his hands together as he watched. "Mr. Jack," he said, "you've got to tell him to stop."

"He won't listen, boy," Jack said. His deep voice was worried, but his hands still worked gently at the bear's neck. The other forestmen stood close behind him, shuffling and muttering.

"*Tell* him," Nick shouted. "Use your magic."

"I tell him with my hands," Jack said. "That is my magic. But sometimes he is wild." He added unhappily, "I am sorry, boy. Bears and forestmen do not understand humans."

Nick had already pulled off his jacket and shirt, and now he ripped the shirt to strips and wrapped them around his hands. "Grandpa, I'm going to try to pull its jaws apart."

"No," Tom said. "I don't want you hurt. Go down and get your father."

"I'm going to do this, Grandpa," Nick said. "When I do, roll out of the way. Excuse me, Mr. Jack."

"This is not good, boy," Jack said. "He will scratch you."

But Nick had already moved around behind the bear and had stepped over its shoulders. He reached with both arms around its neck from behind, worked his wrapped fingers in between its front teeth, and then yanked the jaws apart with all his strength. The bear roared and reared upright on its hind legs. Tom rolled free. Nick wrapped his legs around the bear's middle and rode it for a moment, hugging its shoulders with his elbows to avoid its churning claws. Then the bear lost its balance and began tottering sideways. Afraid of being bitten if he relaxed his grip and let go, Nick still held the bear's jaws as he jumped off its back. His weight pulled the animal over backwards with him, so that it crashed on its side beside the foundation, with its claws clutching the air. Wheezing hoarsely, it rolled desperately back and forth, tossing its head to try to fling Nick off.

Now Nick suddenly tore his hands free, and the motion sent him stumbling backwards into the foundation. He quickly picked himself up and squatted on a floor joist, shaking a little, but ready to clamber away from the bear if it chased after him. Then he saw the bear had not even stood up. It lay on its side. As Nick watched, the bear squealed softly, groaned, and was still.

Tom and the forestmen stood in a circle around the bear and the foundation. "Nick!" Tom called. "For God's sake, are you all right?"

"Yes . . . except my hands. I can't move my fingers." Holding his hands up out of the way, he sidled unsteadily between the joists towards the cellar wall. He noticed, frowning with puzzlement, that the joists split if he pressed against them. "This lumber is awfully flimsy, Grandpa." He climbed up carefully to the ground, shuddering a little. Tom had picked up Nick's jacket, and he laid it now over the boy's bare shoulders. Nick said, "I'm glad you can still use your arm."

"He didn't bite me hard," Tom said. "He keeps his temper better than a certain old fool I know. . . . Now if you can walk all right, we need to get down the hill."

"I can walk," Nick said. "It's just my hands." He looked at the bear and frowned, saying, "He's really hurt, though. Whatever I did, Mr. Jack, I didn't mean to."

"It was my fault again, dad blast it," Tom said. "I'm right sorry, Mr. Jack. I'll try to find the River Spirit for you."

"See, old man." Jack pointed down the cart track. A circle of light was gliding up the hill.

"Tom?"

It was the River Spirit's voice.

"Tom Terry?"

She was walking up the track towards the clearing. Light glimmered from her blue robes to show her way. Theodore was kick-walking up the hill beside her.

"It's a good thing we got here before you dad-blasted yourself into the hereafter," Theodore remarked to Tom, by way of greeting.

"I'm very glad to see you, sir, and you, too, ma'am," Tom said, a little weakly.

"Hmph," said Theodore. "Just show us where the damage is." He hopped ahead of the River Spirit and onto the foundation wall, then waved his paws outwards to the crowd of forestmen and bears. "Back up, everyone," he ordered. "The Princess will need room."

The River Spirit strode forward into the clearing, calling, "Greetings,

Jack Pine. Greetings, everyone." The forestmen all backed up and lowered their heads for a moment; the bears grunted softly. The River Spirit stood before Tom and laid her right hand on his forehead. "You can stop being angry now," she said.

The touch of her palm sent calm like a cool current through him. His anger left him. Sadness remained. "I've been angry about being old, Princess," he said.

She held Tom's wrist between her hands, and the bleeding stopped where the bear's jaws had held him. The pain was gone. "You'll be all right, old friend. I think you'll know what to do now." Before Tom had time to ask her what she meant, she turned and called, "Nick?"

"Yes, ma'am," Nick said. He walked over to her a little awkwardly, as if he wasn't quite sure what he should be doing with his arms and legs.

"Don't be nervous, young man," Theodore said, rather sharply, from his perch on the foundation.

Smiling, the River Spirit asked, "Do you know who I am?"

"Yes, ma'am."

"Let me see those hands." She unwrapped the tatters of his shirt from them, then turned his hands palms up. The bear's teeth had bitten them nearly through. The River Spirit laid her hands over Nick's for a long minute, then squeezed his knuckles between her fingers. Her hands half disappeared into his flesh. "Move your fingers now," she said. They moved easily. "Good. Now I want you to move that bear away from the foundation and put him on flat ground for me. And watch you pick him up gently. Your strength has come in."

"My strength?" he repeated.

"Didn't your grandpa tell you stories about being strong when he was a boy, Nick?"

"Grandma used to tell us — how it cut way back on the chores."

"You have it now," she said. "You can move the bear for me while he's still unconscious."

"Are you kidding? That bear must weigh a thousand pounds."

"The Princess never *kids*," Theodore said. "Do as she told you."

Nick squatted down beside the bear again, shoved his hands and arms wide apart underneath its body, and lifted it up easily. "Where shall I put him?"

"Over here by me."

The bear as he held it was blocking his sight, so he hoisted it over his head. As he walked over to the River Spirit, bears and forestmen backed away from him. He lowered the injured bear to his waist, bent over, and laid the animal at the River Spirit's feet. "Thank you, Nick," she said.

Tom rubbed the back of his neck and shook his head. "This is going to be a bushel of trouble for his mother."

Gathering the folds of her robes and sweeping them behind her, the River Spirit knelt beside the bear. She moved her hands lightly over its back, spread her fingers around its neck and jaws, then circled her palms over its heart. "I want no more racing with this bear. Remember that, would you, Jack?"

"The old forestman and his old bear will retire together, I think," Jack said. "My son can win races now."

"It's nice to know *some* people have sense in their heads," Theodore remarked.

Tom had been standing at the edge of the clearing. He was looking at the flat halfway down the hill, and farther below at his farm, at the faint shimmer of his wheat fields in the starlight, and at the dark river glinting among the cottonwoods. His anger seemed distant now, and foolish. He didn't want it anymore. Peace would suit a man better — and the quiet of remembering the years by the river. He noticed then that Jack and the others were silent behind him, waiting. Turning around to them, he cleared his throat and hooked his thumbs in his suspenders. "I've been thinking, Mr. Jack, that Nick and I might build this house of ours in a different spot. Right here might be a little in your way, and it ain't near enough to water. I've got my eye on that flat halfway down where the creek comes out of the trees." He snapped his suspenders to his chest. "Now, when's the next bear race?"

Jack's black eyes sparked in the night. "At the half moon. We thank you, old man."

"No need to mention it. The half moon . . . that'll be the fifteenth. If Nick will be so kind as to pull up the joists and cinder blocks — which, if I ain't mistaken, he'll have done in half a morning, and without the bother of a crowbar — I'd say we'll have the foundation moved out of here and your race-course set to rights with a week to spare."

"Your grandson can learn to race," Jack said. "But gently, I think."

"That'll be up to his mother."

The River Spirit stood up. Jack nudged the bear's shoulders with his foot. "Old bear, wake up." Snorting and tossing its head, the bear twisted itself to its feet. Jack stepped over its back and tapped its neck with his hand. The other forestmen, too, mounted their bears. Then, swaying their shoulders and kicking out lazily, as their bears ambled with wagging behinds, the spirits rode across the clearing and disappeared into the forest.

Nick pointed. "Look, Grandpa. The River Spirit, too." A circle of light was sinking down the hill. It glimmered a moment at a turn in the cart track and was gone.

"They never stay for small talk, Nick."

The river of stars flowed high overhead now; below, its diamond current glittered on the Cannonball.

"I never stayed up this late before," Nick said.

"We'd best get down to bed before your parents wake up. I'm a mite worn out for the necessary explanations."

"Bed? Are you kidding? I couldn't sleep now. I'm getting started on moving the foundation. I want my own room to sleep in by tomorrow night."

Nick didn't finish his acquaintance with the couch in the farmhouse kitchen in just one day. Things don't go as fast as young people generally want them to. Still, he ended up with his own room in the farmhouse and a sleeping porch in the new house, which was easy to arrange, since he mostly built the new house himself. The bears often lumbered down to the flat to watch, and when they felt like it, they helped out by carrying lumber. You can still see their teeth marks on the door frame, if you look when the light is right. As for Tom, he stepped aside and let Nick design the place with Orville as they pleased.

He said if a man was going to retire and be done with aggravation, he ought to keep his hands off things and let them go.

After the house was built, Tom remembered Nick's talk about the woods as a fine place for the imagination. He asked Jack's permission concerning the bear paths, which twisted and circled through the forest like a maze. Nick sawed out any dead branches that might stab a man's eye, and Tom took to walking the paths at night, if the bears weren't running. He missed the river now and then, and sometimes, right after sunset, whenever he had a mind to hear the water's laughter, you could see him riding on a bear down the hill to the riverbank. But mostly he was happy to lose himself among the trees, just content to hear the creaking of the branches and to listen to the whisper of the pine needles, and the night talk of the animals, and the dark silence.